# FLIGHT 094

DAVIT SHYAM

"A special thanks to Vats Kaushik."

# Contents

# Contents

"To the dreamers, the storytellers, and the quiet souls
Who find magic in words."

It was nearly dusk, and the sky had taken on a deep shade of purple, blending into the horizon. The cabin lights were faint, casting a muted glow that mirrored the stillness of the sleeping passengers. A soft, purple strip of LED lighting ran along the ceiling, giving the space a serene, almost surreal calm. A few reading lamps flickered on, illuminating scattered seats, while most of the travelers were fast asleep, cocooned in their own worlds. Along the gallery floor, thin strips of fluorescent lights stretched toward the exits, barely noticeable but ever-present.

Outside, the two colossal Rolls-Royce engines growled steadily, one mounted on each wing, a low hum of power vibrating through the aircraft. The red and green navigation lights blinked rhythmically on the wings, their glow piercing the darkness. Above, the moon emerged from behind a curtain of clouds, casting a pale reflection on the cloudscape below, painting the aircraft in an ethereal silver light.

Bill sat in his aisle seat, half awake, his head nodding forward from exhaustion. It had been an unbearably long journey, two days of near-constant flying across time zones. Now, finally, he was on his way home. He sat just above the plane's wings, from where he had a partial view of the vast sky outside. In the dim cabin, he could make out the cabin crew chatting quietly near the coffee station by the cockpit, their hushed voices mingling with the soft hum of the engines. The middle seat beside him was empty, and the woman at the window was curled up, peacefully asleep, oblivious to the world around her.

In front of Bill was a cup of coffee, the kind he liked—hot, with plenty of milk. Steam rose lazily from the surface, spiraling upward before dissipating into the cool air. He took a slow sip, savoring the warmth as it traveled down his throat, momentarily relaxing him. His eyes wandered from the coffee to the aisle, and then he glanced out the window, gazing at the moonlit clouds. His body settled back into the seat, his eyelids growing heavy once more.

Suddenly, a deafening bang shattered the The entire plane jolted violently, throwing Bill wide awake. The aircraft lurched sharply to the left, sending the passengers into a panic. His coffee cup was hurled into the air, its contents forming weightless droplets splattered in all directions. The woman beside him screamed as sheer terror spread through the cabin. Bill's heart raced, his pulse thundering in his ears, when, in an instant, a blinding flash of light illuminated the sky outside his window. And then, all went black.

A shrill, high-pitched noise pierced his ears, drowning out every other sound. Bill felt his body yanked backward by an unseen force as if the cabin itself had become a vortex. His seat buckled firmly and held him in place as the aircraft's pressure dropped sharply. For a moment, he was paralyzed, gasping for breath, his senses overwhelmed by the chaos around him.

The plane was still airborne, but barely. The tail section had been torn apart, leaving a gaping hole at the back of the cabin. Wind howled through the void, and a fiery glow engulfed the rear of the plane. The stench of burning metal and fuel filled the air. Passengers, screaming in terror, were sucked toward the opening, helplessly flailing in the zero-gravity-like environment. Blood spattered the walls, and the floor—a grotesque testament to the violence that had just unfolded.

Bill clung to the seat in front of him, pulling himself forward with every ounce of strength he could muster. He had to move, had to reach the cockpit. His fingers dug into the fabric of the seats as he crawled, the pressure around him making every movement feel impossibly heavy. Suddenly, the overhead luggage compartment above him burst open, and a suitcase flew out, crashing into his head with brutal force. His vision blurred, and his body was flung backward, slamming into a nearby seat.

Dazed, he blinked and tried to regain focus. Beside him, a body hung limp, still strapped into its seatbelt. Bill recoiled in horror—the body was headless, a grotesque stump where the neck had been. His stomach lurched, but he forced himself to push on.

His foot was tangled in the seatbelt, and he wrestled with it, finally freeing himself from its grip.

With every ounce of will, he crawled toward the cockpit. Bodies lay strewn across the aisles, some lifeless, others moaning in agony. He was almost there, mere feet away from the door. His hand gripped the edge of a seat as he pulled himself upright. The cockpit door loomed in front of him, closed tight. One of the flight attendants lay dead just beside it, her eyes wide open in a frozen scream.

Bill braced himself and shoved against the door. The pressure inside the cockpit resisted him, but he pushed harder, his desperation outweighing his exhaustion. With one final effort, the door gave way, and he stumbled inside, collapsing onto the floor.

Blood trickled down his face, and his vision swam, but he forced himself to stand. The sight before him was a nightmare—the pilots were dead, their bodies slumped over the controls. The instrument panel flashed with dozens of warnings, alarms blaring incessantly. Through the windshield, the ground loomed closer, rushing toward the plane at a terrifying speed. There was nothing he could do. The end was inevitable.

Bill's breath caught in his throat. His body jolted upright, soaked in sweat. His heart raced as he scanned his surroundings, disoriented. Moonlight streamed through the bedroom curtains, the soft breeze swaying them gently. The room was still. No flashing alarms, no screams, just the distant bark of his neighbor's dog.

Bill exhaled shakily, wiping the cold sweat from his brow.

"Was it the same?" Luna's voice came from the other side of the bed, soft but concerned.

"Yes," Bill muttered, his voice barely a whisper in the dark. He nodded, though she couldn't see it. "The same dream."

# I

# Chapter 1

**"Dad, your coffee," Luna called from the kitchen,**

her voice carrying a lightness that contrasted with the silence of the house. She was dressed in her neatly pressed school uniform, almost ready for another day at high school. It was a typical midweek morning, and the world outside was already in motion.

Luna moved gracefully around the kitchen; her long hair tied back into a scarf. Her hands gently watered the flowers she had planted on the windowsill. She gazed out for a moment, taking in the warmth of the sunny morning. The sky was clear, and the forecast on the television near the dining table predicted more warm days ahead. Birds chirped in the garden, fluttering between branches, and the neighbor's dog barked at the occasional passerby.

Bill entered the kitchen, tugging at his tie, trying to straighten it beneath his collar. The golden stripes on his shoulders gleamed against his crisp white shirt, catching the sunlight that streamed through the window. His name, Bill Richers, stood out boldly on the badge over his heart, the letters in shimmering gold font. He was a large, healthy man, his presence commanding attention. A retired Air Force pilot, now flying commercial airliners, Bill carried the air of someone who had spent years defying gravity.

Despite being in his late forties, Bill looked strikingly young—his face still radiated the energy of someone much younger, and his fitness was evident in his firm, muscular build. Few believed he had a sixteen-year-old daughter. Luna, his pride and joy, was equally captivating. Her green eyes sparkled with life, framed by her long lashes and cheeks that naturally blushed a delicate shade of red. She was as kind as she was beautiful, the kind of girl whose smile could light up a room. Yet, despite her warmth and beauty, she had few friends at school and spent much of her time alone. Her world, for the most part, revolved around her father.

Bill sat at the corner of the dining table, the newspaper in one hand, a steaming cup of coffee in the other. His eyes scanned the headlines, while Luna bustled around the kitchen.

"Did anyone come to check the phone? It's been dead since last week, and I do get important calls on it," Bill asked, still engrossed in the newspaper, barely looking up.

"I don't think anyone did," Marla replied, her voice steady as she served breakfast and continued with the dishes. Marla had been a constant in their home since Luna's mother had passed away. She was older than Bill, and though she was just the housekeeper, she had become much more—a caretaker, a silent guardian of the family's daily rhythm.

Bill sipped his coffee, glancing at his iPad for the morning's emails. He didn't notice the look on Luna's face as she sat down at the table. Her voice broke the quiet hum of the morning.

"Dad, you remember tomorrow is my birthday, right?" she asked softly, her tone full of expectation.

Bill nodded, his attention still half on the screen. "Of course, dear. How could I forget?" he said absentmindedly, the way one might respond when not fully engaged.

"So... we're still going to the beach tomorrow, right? We planned it last week," Luna pressed, her voice tinged with hope.

There was a pause, the kind that stretches a second too long. Bill's face fell slightly, and he cleared his throat, avoiding her gaze. Just then, Marla interrupted, breaking the tension.

"I've finished everything here, sir. May I leave now? I've got some errands to run at home," she said, her bag already slung over her shoulder as she headed toward the front door.

"Sure, Marla. Thanks," Bill said, glancing up briefly as the door clicked shut behind her.

He sighed and turned back to Luna, but the weight of his next words was already hanging in the air. "I… I can't come tomorrow," he said, his voice quieter now. "I've got a layover in LA today, and I won't be back until late tomorrow."

Luna's expression dropped instantly, her face betraying the disappointment she tried to hide. She stared at her half-empty plate, pushing the food around with her fork.

Bill glanced at his watch, sensing the shift in the air but unsure how to fix it. "We're running late for school," he said, standing up. "Come on, let's go. We'll swing by your favorite ice cream place on the way."

He helped Luna with her school bag, grabbing the car keys from the wall hanger by the door. He locked up the house, and when he turned, Luna was already seated in the car, her face turned away, looking out the window. She hadn't said a word since they left the kitchen.

The drive to school was quiet, the tension hanging between them like a fog. Even the promise of her favorite ice cream didn't lift her mood. Luna sat silently, her thoughts far away. Bill felt a pang of guilt but didn't know what to say to make it better. He loved her more than anything, but the demands of his job were relentless.

They pulled up in front of the school gate, and Luna got out without a word. Bill watched her walk away, waiting for her to turn around and wave like she always did. But today, she didn't. The small gesture that had always connected them, even in the briefest moments, was missing. Bill's heart sank as he realized just how much his absence tomorrow would hurt her.

He sat there for a moment longer, staring at the school gates. A deep sigh escaped his lips as he watched Luna disappear inside. The weight of his job, his responsibilities, and the distance growing between him and his daughter pressed heavily on his shoulders.

# II
# Chapter 2

**The party had stretched late into the night.**

Now, only a few stragglers remained, and the alley was nearly empty, shrouded in the quiet stillness of the midnight hour. The once lively atmosphere had dissolved into soft murmurs and the occasional clink of glasses being cleared away.

"The food was too good," Leo chuckled, rubbing his stomach as he let out a contented belch. His laughter was contagious, and Bill and Lucia burst out laughing with him. The three friends walked toward their cars, the night air cool and crisp around them.

Leo veered off toward his car, parked a few steps away. "See you two lovebirds later!" he called out with a wave, his smile still visible in the dim light. Bill gave a quick nod, but his focus was on Lucia, who was settling into the passenger seat beside him. Bill slipped into the driver's seat, pressing the ignition button. The engine roared to life, its growl cutting through the silence of the night, echoing in the surrounding woods.

Bill guided the car onto the street, glancing in the rearview mirror to see Leo following close behind. As they merged onto the main road, Bill's eyes were drawn to the small doll that sat proudly in the center of the dashboard—a porcelain couple, hand in hand. It was the gift he had given Lucia on her birthday, and the soft lights embedded in it glowed faintly, casting a warm hue in the darkness.

It always brought a smile to his face, a symbol of the affection he held for her.

They drove through the dense woods, the trees towering on either side of the road like silent sentinels, their leaves rustling softly in the breeze. The rhythmic hum of the car's engine filled the space between them as they discussed the evening's party, their laughter lingering in the air.

Out of nowhere, Lucia turned toward him with a playful grin. "By the way… where's my gift?" she teased, extending her hand toward him, her fingers wiggling expectantly.

Bill's heart skipped a beat. A bead of sweat formed on his brow, and he quickly wiped it away, trying to play it cool. "What do you mean? What gift?" he stammered, shifting nervously in his seat.

"I know it's in your pocket," Lucia teased further, her eyes sparkling with mischief.

Bill was taken aback. "How did you…?" He paused, unable to finish the sentence, the surprise evident on his face.

Lucia smiled knowingly. "I know everything about you, Bill," she said with a soft chuckle, her voice filled with affection. Without warning, she playfully lunged forward, reaching for his coat pocket.

"No… no… wait!" Bill protested, trying to stop her, but Lucia was determined. Her fingers found the small box hidden deep inside his pocket. Triumphantly, she pulled it out, her eyes wide with curiosity.

Bill's heart raced. His palms felt damp as he watched her slowly untie the ribbon around the box. He was bracing himself, unsure of how she would react. His breath hitched in his throat as she gently opened the box, revealing the ring inside—a delicate blue diamond shimmering in the moonlight that streamed through the car windows.

Lucia's eyes widened, her expression softening as she stared at the ring. Bill, unable to look, squeezed his eyes shut, preparing for… well, he wasn't sure what he was preparing for.

There was a long, quiet pause.

And then, he felt her move.

Bill opened one eye cautiously, just in time to see Lucia slipping the ring onto her finger, her cheeks flushed a delicate pink. The blue diamond caught the moon's glow, sending small beams of light dancing around the car's interior.

Before Bill could react, Lucia threw herself into his arms, wrapping him in a tight embrace. Her warmth, her presence—it was everything he had ever wanted. He held her close, letting the moment wash over him, his heart swelling with love.

But just as he started to lose himself in the quiet joy of the moment, something outside caught his eye. A sudden flash of light—a glaring beam growing larger in the rearview mirror.

His instincts kicked in, but it was too late. The beam of light surged toward them at an alarming speed, closing the distance in seconds.

"Lucia!" Bill shouted, panic flooding his voice.

The world tilted violently as the car was hit with a deafening crash from Lucia's side. The impact was brutal. Bill's body lurched forward, his head slamming into the steering wheel with a sickening thud. Pain shot through his skull as the car spun out of control, flipping into the air like a ragdoll. For a moment, everything seemed to slow down—Bill could feel the weightlessness, hear the terrifying silence before the inevitable fall.

Then, with a thunderous bang, the car slammed into the ground, rolling violently. Glass shattered, metal twisted, and the shriek of grinding steel filled the air as the car tumbled before finally crashing to a halt, upside down, wedged against a large tree.

A thick silence followed, broken only by the faint trickle of liquid. Blood. It dripped steadily from a gash in the door, pooling in the mossy ground beneath the car.

Bill's vision blurred. His mind was spinning, trying to piece together what had just happened. He could feel the warmth of blood trickling down his forehead. He blinked, dazed and disoriented. His body ached, pinned awkwardly between the seat and the crushed steering wheel.

But suddenly, everything shifted.

Bill found himself back in his car, parked in front of his daughter's school. He gasped, breathing heavily, his heart pounding in his chest. It was over. Just another one of those memories. One of the worst memories that haunted him, playing over and over in his mind like a broken record.

He wiped the cold sweat from his brow, his hands trembling as he clutched the steering wheel. The nightmare lingered at the edges of his consciousness, refusing to let go.

But it was just that—a memory. A haunting, inescapable memory.

# III

# Chapter 3

**Bill drove into the airport parking lot,**

the hum of his car engine fading into the quiet darkness as he pulled into his spot. The lot was nearly deserted, its silence broken only by the occasional sound of distant engines revving or tires squealing. The fluorescent lights overhead cast long shadows, making the place feel eerily still.

Stepping out of the car, Bill locked the door with a sharp beep. The sound echoed through the cavernous lot, bouncing off concrete walls and pillars as if the empty space was amplifying the solitude. He rechecked the door handles, a force of habit, ensuring they were securely locked before heading toward the lift.

He pressed the elevator button, and it lit up beneath his finger. The familiar ding of the arriving lift sounded, and the doors slid open with a soft hiss, revealing an empty interior. A light melody played inside—a cheery tune he had heard countless times. Bill couldn't help but whistle along, a quiet, absentminded whistle that filled the small space as the lift ascended.

Pulling out his phone, he quickly typed out a message to Luna. His thumb hovered over the send button for a moment longer than necessary before he hit send. The reply didn't come right away, and Bill's eyes lingered on her profile picture—a bright smile that always brought him a quiet sense of warmth.

Ding.

The lift chimed again as it reached his floor. Bill slid his phone back into his pocket and straightened up as the doors opened to a completely different world.

The airport was alive with motion. The previously still night was now replaced by the bustling, organized chaos of one of the world's busiest terminals. People swarmed the area, moving in every direction, their faces a mix of excitement, exhaustion, and anticipation. The distant hum of announcements echoed through the vast hall, barely discernible over the constant chatter of thousands of voices.

Through the large glass panels, Bill could see planes lined up on the tarmac, waiting for their turn to take off. The runway shimmered in the heat of the lights, and the distant roar of engines filled the air as jets lifted off, disappearing into the night sky. Luggage trucks crisscrossed the tarmac, their flashing lights and beeping horns adding to the symphony of activity.

Buses ferried passengers to planes, while pushback tractors moved massive aircraft into position with a low mechanical rumble. Technicians worked under the wings, their yellow vests glowing under the floodlights as they conducted final inspections.

Inside the terminal, the sea of travelers was no less chaotic. Families, solo travelers, and businessmen all jostled for space, clutching boarding passes and pulling wheeled suitcases. Some crowded around check-in counters, attendants peeling stickers from machines and attaching them to bags with swift precision.

Others sat slumped in the rows of seats, eyes on the screens in front of them, waiting for their boarding call. The lines at the security checkpoints snaked far back, inching forward at a painfully slow pace.

Bill flashed his ID to a security guard who waved him through. The metal detector's wand beeped as it scanned his body, but the guard handed his ID back without a word. Once through, the crowds thinned slightly, though the air was still thick with movement and sound.

Flight attendants, dressed in crisp uniforms and brightly colored scarves, huddled together in groups, chatting and laughing softly near the gates. Armed security officers patrolled the perimeter with trained dogs, their eyes scanning the throngs of people for anything suspicious.

The sight of the officers always brought a small twinge of unease to Bill's stomach, a remnant of his days in the Air Force.

He sidestepped a group of children running through the terminal, their laughter high-pitched and infectious as they darted between travelers. An older couple was slowly pushed through the crowds in wheelchairs, their faces serene in the midst of the hustle.

The scent of coffee and freshly baked pastries wafted from nearby cafés, mingling with the sharper smells of jet fuel and disinfectant.

Bill found himself gravitating toward one of the coffee stands, the soft hiss of steam escaping from the machines enticing him. The barista handed him a cup, and Bill wrapped his hands around it, the warmth seeping through his fingers. He took a slow sip, the familiar taste comforting in the chaos around him.

As he walked, he noticed a young woman nearby, struggling to calm her crying baby. Her voice was soft, almost musical, as she tried to hush the infant, rocking him gently in her arms. The scene tugged at something deep inside Bill, stirring a memory.

He could almost see Lucia, her soothing voice cradling Luna to sleep in those quiet moments of the night. The way she used to sing, her voice full of love and tenderness, could always calm Luna in an instant.

For a moment, Bill stood still, lost in the memory. The warmth from his coffee faded as his thoughts drifted back to those late-night lullabies. A sharp pang of loss twisted in his chest, the kind of ache that never really goes away.

He shook himself from the reverie, taking a deep breath. The noise of the airport rushed back in, reminding him where he was. He adjusted his sunglasses as if trying to shield himself from the emotions threatening to surface. With a quiet resolve, he turned away from the young mother and continued his walk through the terminal, blending into the crowd as if nothing had happened.

But inside, the memories clung to him, as persistent as the hum of the airport around him.

# IV

## Chapter 4

**The sharp ring of the school bell echoed down the corridor,** and within seconds, the once-quiet hallway was filled with the sound of chattering students, their footsteps a chaotic rhythm on the polished floor. Luna, moving slower than usual, packed her bag while her friends waited outside the classroom door.

Amelia and Ron were her closest friends, though in truth, Luna had never been one to keep a large circle. Amelia, always full of energy, was Luna's confidante, while Ron, with his easy-going nature, was the one who quietly made sure she was never alone.

As Luna stepped out of the classroom, Amelia immediately bounded over, throwing her arms around her in a tight hug. "Lunaaa!" she exclaimed, but Luna barely reacted, her mind was somewhere else. Amelia's face fell slightly, concerned, as Luna walked past, her steps slow and distracted.

"What's wrong, Luna?" Amelia asked, her voice softening. Luna didn't respond, her eyes focused ahead as she descended the stairs. Ron, walking beside them, could tell something was off.

He leaned over and whispered to Amelia, who nodded thoughtfully. They both stopped Luna at the bottom of the stairs. "Will you go for ice cream?" Ron asked, his voice gentle and hopeful. He knew her too well—ice cream was her kryptonite. Luna could never say no to it, no matter how bad her mood was.

Luna paused, as if weighing the offer, before giving the smallest of nods and heading toward the park.

The three of them sat on a bench in the nearby park, shaded by tall trees that swayed lazily in the breeze. The distant sound of children playing and birds chirping filled the air, a contrast to the quiet tension in their group.

Luna licked her ice cream absentmindedly, her gaze distant as if lost in thought. Beside her, Ron was making a mess, chocolate ice cream smeared comically around his lips, with melted drops pooling on his hands. Amelia, ever the neat eater, took delicate bites of her vanilla cone while keeping one eye on Luna.

Even as she ate, Luna's usual spark was missing. She sat there, quiet and withdrawn, a stark contrast to her usual chatty self. Amelia leaned in, speaking softly, trying to coax something out of her.

After a few attempts, Luna finally spoke, her voice low. "It's just... Dad won't be home for my birthday. Again." Her words were clipped, barely hiding the disappointment that weighed heavily on her.

Ron, overhearing the conversation as he wiped the melted ice cream from his hand, understood immediately. Luna's father, Bill, meant the world to her. She'd been looking forward to spending her birthday with him, but now, those plans were slipping through her fingers.

Once they'd finished their ice creams, Amelia excused herself for her music class, leaving Ron to walk Luna home. The sun had started to dip lower in the sky, casting a golden glow over the park as they made their way through the familiar streets.

Ron moved closer to her, sensing the need to break the silence. "So," he began, his tone light, "did I tell you about how I nearly knocked over the lab equipment today in chemistry? Mrs. Henderson gave me that 'I know it was you'd look, but I totally played it off." He chuckled, trying to get a reaction out of her.

Luna gave a small smile but didn't say much. Not one to give up easily, Ron pressed on, recounting stories from their day, slowly drawing her out. "Remember that guy in history who's always asleep? Today, he actually snored loud enough to wake himself up. Funniest thing ever!"

That did the trick. Luna giggled, and once she started, she couldn't stop. She launched into her own story, talking about how she hid a broken test tube in chemistry without getting caught. As they walked, their conversation flowed easily, and by the time they reached Luna's house, she was laughing and talking like her usual self.

Ron was glad to see her smile again, but he knew that her sadness about her father lingered beneath the surface. He walked her to the door, waiting until she was safely inside before heading back home.

Inside, Marla was already busy preparing lunch, her back turned as she stirred something on the stove. Luna greeted her with a tired smile and headed straight to her room, where she fell onto her bed, the weight of her disappointment creeping back in now that she was alone.

Later that night, Ron lay on his bed, staring up at the ceiling. He couldn't stop thinking about Luna—how sad she'd been, how much her father's absence was hurting her. He knew how important birthdays were to her, and how much she looked forward to spending them with her dad.

"I need to do something," he muttered to himself, his mind racing for a plan. But what could he do? How could he possibly make up for Bill's absence?

As he lay there, his phone buzzed on his nightstand. It was a text from Amelia. Any news from Luna? She's not answering my calls.

Ron picked up his phone and quickly typed back. Yeah, I talked to her. She's really down about her dad not being home for her birthday. Marla said she went to bed early.

A few seconds later, Amelia's reply came through: We've got to do something for her. She deserves better than spending her birthday feeling like this.

Ron stared at the screen, Amelia's words echoing what he had already been thinking. Then, suddenly, an idea flashed into his mind.

He shot up in bed, excitement bubbling up in his chest as he grabbed his phone and quickly dialed Amelia's number. The phone rang twice before she picked up.

"Amelia, I've got a plan," Ron said, his voice brimming with enthusiasm. "But I'm going to need your help."

# V

# Chapter 5

**Bill walked into the airline office,**
a sprawling, bustling space alive with the hum of computers and the murmur of voices. Employees sat behind screens, fingers tapping away at keyboards, while others held quiet, focused conversations on the phones at their desks. The room smelled faintly of coffee and fresh paper, a familiar scent that always reminded Bill he was back in his element.

He moved toward his usual table, where a thick stack of documents awaited him. Without wasting any time, Bill began flipping through the pages. His eyes skimmed the familiar flight routes and technical checklists, his mind on autopilot. He scribbled his name at the bottom of each page, the pen scratching quietly as he completed his task.

Once done, he handed the papers to the man seated across from him—one of the flight coordinators—before heading to another room for his routine health checkup. These were always quick and thorough, something Bill had done so many times it felt more like a formality. A few minutes later, he was back in the office, where his flight details and updated papers were waiting.

With everything in order, Bill pulled his suitcase behind him and made his way toward the boarding gate. The sun was setting, casting the sky in hues of deep orange and gold, its last light disappearing slowly behind the horizon. The soft glow of dusk bathed the airport in a quiet beauty. Bill paused for a moment, taking in, the sense of calm before the journey ahead.

As he walked through the aero bridge, he instinctively reached for his phone to call Luna, as he did before every flight. He dialed her number, but after a few rings, it went unanswered. Bill's heart sank a little, knowing she was still upset about her birthday.

He sighed, then opened a voice message. "Sorry, dear. Forgive your daddy this time. I promise we'll go anywhere you want next week. Just hang in there, okay?" He sent the message, feeling a pang of guilt, then turned on airplane mode as he approached the aircraft.

The air hostesses greeted him with smiles as he boarded. "Captain," they said warmly, and Bill returned the smiles with a polite nod. His first officer, a young recruit with eager eyes, followed him into the cockpit. Bill could see the mixture of excitement and nerves on the man's face; it was a look he remembered having himself, long ago.

Night had fully fallen by the time the plane began to taxi down the runway. The hum of the engines intensified, and soon, the aircraft was slicing through the sky, leaving behind the sparkling lights of the city below.

From the cockpit, the world looked different—a sea of shimmering lights that twinkled like stars against the earth. As they ascended above the clouds, the sky took on a serene orange hue, where the moon and stars were beginning to glow, casting a soft light over the darkening world.

The flight was smooth and uneventful. The weather all the way to Los Angeles was calm, with barely any turbulence. Bill flew with the practiced ease of someone who had spent decades in the air. Each maneuver was precise, each decision instinctive.

He always made it a point to land as softly as possible—especially on night flights—so as not to disturb the sleeping passengers. When the plane touched down at LAX, it was with barely a bump, and Bill allowed himself a small smile of satisfaction.

By the time the last passenger disembarked, the airport was nearly empty, and the clock in the cockpit read just past midnight. Bill was one of the last to leave the plane, his steps slow with the fatigue that had begun to settle in. The hot, humid air of Los Angeles greeted him as he stepped outside, a stark contrast to the cool, climate-controlled environment of the aircraft.

As he walked toward the airline office, Bill pulled out his phone to check for any updates from Luna. His message had been delivered, but not read. He frowned, a wave of concern washing over him, but tried to push it aside. She's probably just asleep, he thought.

Inside the office, Bill handed over another set of flight papers before making his way to the taxi that was waiting for him outside. The young driver greeted him with a grin, the car's speakers thumping with the deep bass of some energetic music.

It wasn't exactly Bill's taste, but tonight he didn't mind. He found himself tapping his fingers along with the beat as they drove through the bustling streets of Los Angeles. Despite the late hour, the city was still alive, neon lights flashing from the buildings and pedestrians still milling about on the sidewalks.

The drive took about half an hour, with the vibrant city gradually giving way to quieter, residential areas. When they finally pulled up to the hotel, Bill thanked the driver, grabbed his luggage, and headed inside. The receptionist, a young woman with a tired but friendly smile, handed him his room key and gave him brief directions to the elevator.

Once inside his room, Bill let out a deep breath. The room was dimly lit, with soft ambient lighting along the ceiling giving it a warm, inviting glow. He hung his coat on the rack and kicked off his shoes before heading to the bathroom to take a long, hot shower.

The steam and heat helped wash away the stress of the flight, but his mind kept drifting back to Luna. He checked his phone again after the shower, hoping to see that she had read his message, but there was still nothing.

Bill sighed, feeling the familiar weight of guilt settle in his chest. He knew he had missed too many birthdays, too many important moments in her life. But flying was in his blood, and sometimes, the balance between being a good father and a good pilot felt impossible to maintain.

After drying off, Bill slipped into his pajamas and climbed into the large, comfortable bed. The air conditioning hummed softly, cooling the room to just the right temperature. He pulled the blanket up to his chin, enjoying the comforting weight of it as he sank deeper into the mattress.

The dim lights along the ceiling cast soft shadows across the room, and the quiet was almost serene. Yet, even as his body relaxed, his thoughts stayed on Luna. He stared at his phone one last time before setting it on the bedside table.

"Tomorrow," he muttered to himself, turning over. "I'll make it up to her tomorrow."

Within minutes, the exhaustion of the day caught up with him, and Bill drifted off into a deep, dreamless sleep.

# VI

## chapter 6

**The warm sunlight filtered through the curtains,** casting a golden glow over Luna's bedroom. She was still wrapped under her blanket, only half aware of Marla's lively humming blending with the upbeat jingles from the radio. Marla, always an early riser, had already begun her daily chores, her voice light and cheerful as she moved from room to room.

"Luna, get up! It's already seven," Marla called out, her tone gentle but firm.

Luna groaned softly, rubbing the sleep from her eyes as she reluctantly sat up. She stretched her arms out wide, letting out a big yawn before glancing at her phone on the nightstand. A few missed calls from her dad and Amelia flashed on the screen, along with the usual notifications. Luna sighed and unlocked the phone, scrolling through her messages.

Just as she started to reply, the doorbell rang its sharp chime cutting through the morning stillness. Marla, ever efficient, hurried to answer it. Luna placed her phone back on the bed and slid into her slippers, shuffling toward the living room, her curiosity piqued. She half-expected it to be Ron, maybe stopping by with some morning mischief.

When Marla opened the door, a young man stood on the threshold. He was brown-skinned, with a neatly trimmed beard, wearing a navy blue uniform that marked him as a service technician. A large black tool bag hung from his shoulder, and the emblem on his cap confirmed Luna's guess—he must be here to fix the telephone.

"Good morning! I'm Rafi," the man introduced himself with a polite nod. "I was informed that your telephone has been down for a few days. I'm here to take a look."

Marla, always warm and hospitable, gave him a welcoming smile. "Ah, yes, the telephone! Come right in." She gestured toward the living room. The space was neat and inviting, the morning light making everything look brighter and more colorful.

"Please, make yourself comfortable. I'll be right back," Marla said as she bustled off toward the kitchen, leaving Rafi to settle on the edge of the sofa.

Luna wandered toward the door, picking up the newspaper and magazine that had been dropped off earlier. She glanced at Rafi, who was quietly surveying the room, then disappeared into the kitchen without a word. Marla soon returned with a cup of coffee for their visitor—her natural instinct to treat guests like family showing through. Luna ignored the exchange, lost in her own thoughts.

Opening the fridge, Luna pulled out a bottle of milk and poured herself a cup. The fridge door was a patchwork of memories—family photographs from beach trips and hikes, brightly colored magnets from places she and her father had visited together. Little snippets of the past, all neatly arranged, reminded her of times that felt both close and distant.

She took a slow sip of her milk, flipping absentmindedly through the pages of a magazine while Rafi and Marla spoke in the other room. Marla was explaining the issue, though the man remained mostly quiet, focused on the task ahead.

"Let me show you where the telephone is," Marla said, leading Rafi toward the small rack beside the TV cabinet where the phone was kept. As they passed by the cabinet, Rafi glanced at the medals and trophies proudly displayed—many of them Luna's from her school days, along with a few awards from Bill's youth, all neatly arranged like artifacts in a museum of family achievements.

Rafi set his tool bag down with a soft thud, pulling out a few tools and inspecting the telephone with practiced efficiency. Marla continued her cleaning, occasionally glancing over to check on his progress. Meanwhile, Luna stood by the kitchen door, her eyes flicking between her magazine and the man working in the corner, still somewhat wary of this stranger in their home.

The soft clicks and clicks of Rafi's tools filled the room, blending with Marla's quiet humming. There was something comforting in the routine of it all—the gentle rhythm of an ordinary morning unfolding, even with the unexpected presence of the repairman.

# VII
## Chapter 7

**It was a warm and sunny April morning,**
and the day already promised to be a busy one for Bill. Dressed in his sharp suit, he made his way downstairs from the hotel, where a taxi waited for him at the entrance. With a cup of coffee in hand, he took a quick bite of his breakfast before leaping into the back seat.

The ride to the airport took about half an hour, and as the taxi pulled up, Bill stepped out, tilting his head to glance up at the clear sky through his sunglasses. The sun's rays warmed his skin, but there was a sharpness to them, a sting of heat that made him squint slightly.

As he walked toward the terminal, he pulled out his phone and typed a quick message: "Happy birthday, dear." He hit send, smiling softly to himself as he made his way inside the bustling airport. Stopping at the Starbucks just beyond the entrance, Bill grabbed a second coffee.

He had a long day ahead and would need the extra caffeine. The airport was busy, as always, with a steady stream of travelers moving through security and check-in. Still, everything went smoothly for him until the familiar moment of being stopped by a security guard.

"May I see your bag, please?" the guard asked, motioning for Bill to step aside.

Bill wasn't fazed. It was a routine occurrence—something always seemed to trigger the scanners when he traveled. He took the last sip of his coffee, tossed the empty cup into a nearby trash can, and unzipped his bag. The guard reached in, feeling around carefully.

Just then, Bill's phone rang. An unknown number flashed on the screen. Stepping aside, Bill answered, but there was nothing but silence on the other end. He listened for a moment, then tried to speak again, "Hello? Anyone there?" Still no response.

With a sigh, he hung up, thinking it must be a network issue, and returned to the security check. The guard smiled, holding up a pen. "Just this, sir. Nothing to worry about. You're good to go."

Bill chuckled, relieved. "Thank you," he replied, grabbing his bag off the counter.

"Have a good day," the guard said as Bill walked away toward his gate. There was still some time before boarding, so he decided to browse the airport shops, hoping to find a little gift for Luna. His daughter loved surprises, and he always tried to bring her something back from his trips.

As he wandered, something in the jewelry store caught his eye. The shop's display cases shimmered under the lights, but one particular piece stood out: a pendant in the shape of a crescent moon, delicately carved from a sparkling diamond. Perfect for Luna, he thought with a smile.

He stepped into the store, admiring the pendant up close, and without hesitation, purchased it. The clerk wrapped it in a beautiful, ornate box, and Bill tucked it safely into his bag. It was almost time to board now. The flight had arrived, and Bill picked up his pace, walking briskly toward the gate.

At the boarding gate, the attendant smiled warmly as Bill showed his pass. He pulled his suitcase behind him, making his way across the long glass aero bridge that connected the terminal to the plane. He could see the aircraft—a familiar A321, one that always felt like home to him.

Stepping aboard, Bill was greeted by two flight attendants at the door. Their professional smiles were welcoming, but it was the sight of the crew chief that warmed Bill's heart. Miss Aubrey—Aury, as Bill affectionately called her—was an old friend.

They had known each other for over twenty years. In fact, she had been close friends with his late wife, Lucia, and over the years, Bill had flown with her on countless flights. Aury's daughter, Amelia, and Bill's daughter, Luna, had grown up together and were best friends.

As he made his way to his seat, Bill felt a sense of comfort wash over him. This flight, like so many others, felt like a familiar routine. Yet, with the pendant for Luna safely tucked away in his bag, this trip felt a little more special.

# VIII
## Chapter 8

**Bill handed his coat to Aury with a warm smile before stepping into the cockpit.**

There, the first officer, Leo, was already at his station. Leo had been Bill's closest friend since their youth, and seeing him again felt like a reunion of old times.

"Leo, there you are!" Bill said, flipping through the cockpit checklist. "Where'd you disappear to after the New Year? I didn't expect to have the whole crew together today. How's everything with you?"

Leo grinned, "Good to see you too, Bill. Life's been busy, but it's great to be back up here with you."

As the boarding process began, Bill exited the cockpit for his routine aircraft inspection. Stepping out into the bright sunlight, he shielded his eyes from the harsh rays and began his thorough check of the plane. He examined the exterior for any dents, scratches, or mechanical faults.

For many pilots, this was just a routine, but for Bill, it was akin to a sacred ritual. He placed his hands gently on the engine, closing his eyes in what seemed like a silent prayer to the aircraft.

The plane was in pristine condition: newly painted, with fresh tires, well-greased gears, and no visible damage. Every sensor and hydraulic system functioned perfectly. Satisfied, Bill returned to the cockpit to prepare for the flight. He handed a few documents to Leo, and as he did so, Aury knocked and entered.

"Load reports?" Bill asked as Aury handed over the papers. After a brief review, he noted, "We have 172 souls on board, including our crew. So, we have Carie, Jessica, John, and you on our team today." He checked off items on his checklist and scribbled some details in his notepad before returning the documents to Aury.

"Anything else?" Aury asked, already knowing the answer.

"You know me too well," Bill replied with a chuckle. "One hot coffee with extra cream. And Leo, what about you?"

"Maybe just a green tea," Leo said, flashing a smile.

As the plane was prepared for pushback, Aury closed the aircraft door while a ground staff member gave a friendly wave from outside. She then secured the cockpit door as the plane began its backward maneuver.

Bill picked up the microphone from above and addressed the passengers: "This is your captain Bill welcoming you aboard. We're headed to New York today. The sky is clear, and we expect a smooth flight of approximately six and a half hours. We hope you enjoy the journey. Have a great day."

Bill replaced the mic and turned his attention to the flight controls. "Costal zero-nine-four, you are cleared for takeoff on two-five right," crackled the voice over the headset.

"My controls," Bill said as he pushed the thrust lever to its maximum, lifting the aircraft into the clear blue sky. After a few turns, they reached cruising altitude.

Bill pressed the button labeled AP1, which blinked twice before turning green, indicating the autopilot was engaged. He then turned off the seatbelt sign, unbuckled his seatbelt, and reclined his chair.

Aury entered the cockpit with Bill's coffee and Leo's tea. Bill set his cup on the tray and pulled out his iPad to catch up on some reading. Meanwhile, Aury began preparing the in-flight meals, with Jessica assisting her in making the coffee and serving drinks.

In the rear, John and Carie were busy with meal preparations. Carie, a young woman in her mid-twenties, was new to the team but worked efficiently. John, a seasoned flight attendant with over ten years of experience, had a background in wrestling, which added a unique touch to his approach to the job.

As Bill read through his iPad, he received a notification—an email from Luna. There was no subject or text, just an attached picture. Assuming it might be birthday photos, he tapped on the notification with his touch pen. As the email opened, the content of the photograph made Bill's breath catch in his throat.

He was thrown back into his seat, his hands trembling as his touch pen slipped from his grasp. The image on the screen was shocking, and Bill struggled to process what he saw.

# IX

## Chapter 9

**Bill closed his eyes for a moment,**

hoping to wake up from what felt like a nightmare. But when he opened them, the picture on his iPad was still there. It was a snapshot of his living room—the flat-screen LED TV they had bought just a month ago, the family photos framed and placed around the cabinet, and the familiar fridge adorned with Luna's childhood scribbles. On top of it was the artificial flower vase Luna had crafted in her art class. The shadow of the old oak tree in their garden cast a gentle, nostalgic glow over everything.

Yet, something was profoundly wrong. At the center of the room, on a chair, was a girl whose hands were bound with thick rope. Though her face was obscured, the bracelet on her wrist was unmistakable. It was Luna.

Bill's breath caught in his throat. His heart pounded as he noticed something even more alarming: Luna was dressed in a black jacket, wires of various colors protruding from it. On the jacket's chest were buttons and a small, ominous chip. "Is that a bomb?" Bill whispered, his voice trembling.

Before he could process the horrifying image fully, another email from Luna's account popped up on his screen. This time, it was a video. Bill's hands shook uncontrollably as he fumbled for his earphones in his bag, trying desperately to connect them to his iPad.

He struggled to plug in the metal jack, his fingers slipping with the effort.

Finally, managing to get the earphones in, he glanced around the cockpit. The door behind him was securely closed, and Leo was absorbed in his book, oblivious to Bill's growing panic.

With one earbud in place, Bill tapped the play button, his anxiety escalating as the screen remained blank for a moment. Sweat from his forehead dripped onto the screen.

Suddenly, a face appeared—a young man with curly brown hair and a long beard. He cleared his throat before addressing Bill. "Hey Bill, this is Rafi. I hope you've seen the picture of your daughter.

Doesn't she look beautiful in that jacket? Don't worry, I won't harm her, provided you follow my instructions. And don't even think about alerting anyone. My men are watching you."

The call ended abruptly, leaving Bill in stunned silence. His mind raced. Should he inform Aury? But Rafi's threat about his men being on him suggested there could be threats within the plane itself.

Just then, another call came through—another video call. Without hesitation, Bill answered it, the green button pressing firmly beneath his trembling fingers. The ceiling in the call matched the one in his living room. The same man, Rafi, appeared on the screen.

"If you're as clever as I think you are, you're probably doubting the authenticity of the video," Rafi began, his tone almost mocking. "So I thought I'd make it more convincing."

Bill opened his mouth to speak, but no words came out. He glanced nervously at Leo, who remained engrossed in his book. Bill turned back to the screen and typed quickly, "Show me Luna."

"Smart," Rafi replied with a smirk. He lifted the phone and walked through the room, the camera swaying with his movement. Bill's dread grew as he confirmed that this was indeed his home.

Rafi finally turned the camera towards Luna. He slowly removed the mask from her face. Luna's eyes were wide with fear as she looked into the camera. Her mouth was sealed with duct tape. As Rafi pulled the tape away, Luna's voice, though strained and desperate, reached Bill's ears. "DADDY," she cried out.

Bill's heart shattered at the sight of his daughter in such distress. Before he could react, the screen went black, and a message appeared: "Call ended." Bill was left staring at the blank screen, overwhelmed by a sense of helplessness and terror.

# X
# Chapter 10

**The alarm clock blared incessantly,**

its harsh tones piercing through the stillness of Ron's room. Buried beneath his blanket, Ron groaned and flailed his hand, hitting the top of the clock with a thud. He pulled the covers back over his head, hoping to drown out the sound, but sleep remained elusive.

Moments later, he jolted awake, his body shooting upright as he scrambled for his phone. His heart raced as he turned it on, a flood of notifications inundating the screen: 9 missed calls from Amelia, dozens of messages, and—most importantly—it was Luna's birthday. Panic surged through him as he leaped out of bed, yanking off his nightshirt and rummaging through his closet.

In a frantic rush, he pulled out a suit, deciding on a sharp blue ensemble amidst the chaos of a cluttered room. Struggling with his socks, he stumbled multiple times before finally managing to get dressed.

He dashed to the mirror, quickly combing his hair and slathering on too much gel. In his haste, he nearly emptied half a bottle of perfume over himself. He grabbed his coat and bolted for the door, only to skid to a stop when he realized he'd forgotten his phone and wallet.

Returning to his room, Ron fumbled through a drawer and retrieved an envelope stuffed with cash—savings from his New Year's presents. He stuffed the money into his wallet, shoved it into his coat pocket, and ran back out. Almost immediately, he remembered his phone again and sprinted back to grab it. Finally, with everything in hand, he hurried out to meet Amelia.

Amelia was waiting at the café near the flower shop, her face flushed with frustration. As Ron arrived, she glared at him. "You fool, always late!"

"It's not the time to fight," Ron shot back, out of breath. "We're already running late."

"Late because of you," Amelia retorted, her anger palpable.

After a brief and heated argument, they agreed to buy a bouquet from the flower shop. While the shopkeeper prepared the arrangement, Ron darted to the nearby bakery to pick up a cake. The clock was ticking, and every second counted.

Meanwhile, Bill was still grappling with the shocking revelations. He had nearly slipped into unconsciousness from the stress, but he forced himself to focus on Leo, who was absorbed in his iPad, likely perusing new flight manuals. Bill returned to his own iPad, hoping for any new updates. The email was still the same—no new messages.

Desperate, he decided to make another call. The phone rang but went unanswered. Panic gripped him as he saw a call coming in from Lucia's mobile. Without hesitation, he answered, almost before the call fully connected.

On the screen was Rafi, who appeared to be in the kitchen, preparing something by the oven—likely coffee. Bill's eyes were fixed on the screen as Rafi took a sip from a cup that looked eerily familiar: Bill's personal coffee cup.

Rafi looked directly into the camera; his expression unreadable. "All you need to do is bring the plane down. Not now, but when I tell you."

Bill was paralyzed with shock. He began typing a response but was interrupted by Rafi's cold voice. "I know what you're thinking, but that doesn't concern me. The plan is straightforward.

There's a small pouch in your bag—just mix its contents into your first officer's tea or coffee. Soon, you'll be alone in the cockpit. I've even provided an automatic pistol for your convenience. I trust you know how to use it."

Bill's hands shook as he typed, "What about the passengers?"

Rafi's eyes narrowed. "You shouldn't worry about them right now. Focus on the task at hand: crashing the plane."

"I'm not crashing the plane," Bill typed fiercely. "And you're not doing anything to my daughter."

"That's not an option," Rafi replied coldly. "You must choose: your life or your daughter's."

The call ended abruptly, leaving Bill in a daze, struggling to process the gravity of the situation. He sat motionless, his mind racing. The immediate concern was the safety of the passengers and how he would handle the dire situation Rafi had imposed on him.

# XI
# Chapter11

**Hoffs was deep in concentration in the dim**, cluttered room. The large space was lined with shelves stacked high with files, and maps of the city dotted the walls, marked with various colored circles and pins.

A mind map sprawled across the whiteboard, its chaotic web of words and scribbles detailing ongoing investigations. On the opposite wall, a row of machine guns and trays of bullets were neatly organized, alongside various gun maintenance tools.

Hoffs, a towering figure at six foot two, with a solid, imposing frame, lounged in his armchair, his gaze fixed on the old pistol he was testing. The room echoed with the sharp, staccato sounds of gunfire, each shot reverberating off the walls.

Lara entered, holding a file, and reached for the light switch near the door. The old tube lights flickered several times before casting a harsh glow over the room. "Officer Hoffs," she called out, her voice slicing through the cacophony of gunshots.

Hoffs, engrossed in a first-person shooter game on his PlayStation, quickly paused the game and set the controller aside. He turned his attention to Lara as she laid the file on the table.

Hoffs, with his years of experience in both military and special task forces, had a commanding presence. His reputation for apprehending some of the city's most dangerous criminals preceded him.

Lara, young yet resolute, carried the aura of someone who had quickly adapted to the demands of her role. Her black shirt bore a badge that reflected in the light, while two silver pistols were holstered on her back, and a small pouch on her left thigh held ammunition.

She was someone Hoffs respected not just for her professional acumen but also for her background—her father, a renowned archaeologist, had taken her on many of his expeditions.

"These are the post-mortem reports for the landline worker found in the trash bin two days ago," Lara said, placing the file in front of Hoffs.

Hoffs skimmed through the documents. "It looks like something was mixed into his water. A lethal poison."

Lara nodded. "The water bottle was found with the body, but the forensic report isn't in yet."

"And the body was found naked," Hoffs noted, his brow furrowing. "Any idea why someone would strip him of his uniform?"

"Not yet," Lara replied. "We're also still waiting on details about his van."

Hoffs leaned back in his chair, pulling out his pistol and an extra magazine from his drawer. "We need to check the township area. It's the last known location of the van."

❧

Meanwhile, Ron and Amelia were in a frantic rush towards Luna's house, their patience frayed by the ticking clock. Amelia, holding a large bouquet and a paper bag, and Ron, struggling with a box of cake, were bickering as they approached the house.

Amelia pressed the doorbell repeatedly, growing increasingly agitated as the dog next door barked incessantly from behind the fence. She tried the door handle and found it unlocked. Pushing the door open, she was suddenly met with a huge man who lunged at her, his body a shield against what was about to unfold.

Before Amelia could react, a deafening explosion erupted behind the man. The force of the blast hurled both Amelia and the man out into the yard, the impact sending them crashing against the ground.

The door, blown off its hinges, struck the man with immense force, while Ron, a few steps behind, was flung violently to the far corner of the yard by the explosion.

The scene erupted into chaos, the once calm afternoon shattered by the violence and confusion of the blast.

# XII
## Chapter 12

**The lunch service was nearly underway,** and the cabin buzzed with passengers absorbed in their activities. The man seated in the business class in front of Aury was capturing the expansive blue sky with his camera. As she made her way down the aisle, she noticed passengers engrossed in their infotainment systems—some watching movies, others listening to music, and a few exploring the new features of the plane.

Aury reached the rear of the plane and checked with John. "Are we ready to serve lunch?"

"All ready, ma'am," John replied, securing the last tray in the cart.

"Excellent. We'll start the service soon," Aury said, giving him an encouraging nod.

On her return journey towards the cockpit, Aury glanced at various passengers' screens, ensuring everything was in order. Her attention was abruptly drawn to a screen in the middle seat, directly above the wings. A woman sat by the window engrossed in a book, and the seat next to her was vacant.

The man in the middle seat was watching the news, but it was the images on the screen that made Aury's heart race—Bill's photo appeared.

Aury paused, her heart pounding. Though she couldn't hear the broadcast due to the man's earphones, the sight of the explosion at Bill's house was chilling. Just as she was about to rush to Bill, Amelia's photo flashed on the screen, followed by Ron's.

Her pulse quickened as she hurried to the cockpit, pulling out her phone and knocking urgently on the door. "Bill, Bill, do you hear me? Come out quick!" she called out, her voice filled with urgency.

Bill, his earphones still in place, looked up. "Excuse me for a minute," he said to Leo, pulling out the earphones and setting them on the table. He followed Aury out, confusion evident on his face.

Aury led Bill to a secluded corner between the ovens and the coffee maker. "There's been a blast at your house," she said hurriedly, her anxiety palpable. She glanced at her phone and continued, "Amelia and Ron were there to celebrate Luna's birthday when the explosion happened."

Bill's face went pale. "What about Luna? Is she okay?"

Aury took a deep breath. "Amelia said Luna wasn't home. Ron has a minor fracture and has been taken to the hospital. Officer Hoffs is the one who saved them."

Bill looked devastated. John, noticing the tension, helped Bill into one of the jump seats.

Aury texted Officer Hoffs for more details. As she read the response, her expression shifted to one of confusion. "Officer Hoffs says they didn't find Luna. They found the body of an elderly woman, probably Marla. She was murdered before the blast—stabbed with a knife."

Aury wiped away a tear and added, "Thank God Luna wasn't in the house."

Bill's eyes widened in horror. "The criminal must have taken her. She's been kidnapped." He recounted the entire ordeal to Aury and Jhon.

Aury relayed the information to Officer Hoffs. "They also found the body of a repair person two days ago. He was poisoned by drinking from a bottle with a black label and a joker face."

Bill, who had been holding a water bottle, looked at it in shock. It matched the description perfectly.

"I got it," Bill said, his voice filled with realization and dread.

# XIII

## Chapter 13

**"Flight nine-one-two, maintain an altitude of thirty thousand feet for the next half hour,"**

Sofia's voice rang out through the mic, her hand pressing the blue button to confirm the instruction. A moment later, the pilots of Flight 912 acknowledged the command.

Sofia's control room was a hive of activity, a symphony of beeps and whirs from the array of equipment that filled the space. In front of her, a panel of buttons glowed softly, and four monitors displayed various flight data and radar information.

The central monitor featured a green concentric circle on a grid, with moving dots representing aircraft in the airspace. A pair of binoculars sat on her desk, next to a photo of her young daughter and a collection of aircraft models. The desk was a mix of black telephones, save for one bright red phone that stood out, signaling its importance.

It was a quiet afternoon; the traffic was light, and half of the control room was empty. The remaining controllers were engrossed in their tasks, with two of them using binoculars to observe planes taking off. Sofia absentmindedly played with a model of an A380, trying to ignore the tempting aroma of a hamburger as one of her colleagues indulged in a Happy Meal behind her.

Her gaze shifted to the group of monitors mounted on the ceiling, each displaying different news channels. The screens were filled with the same distressing news: "The car of the pilot whose house exploded a few hours ago was found in the parking lot at JFK International Airport.

Does it contain a bomb? The bomb squad is on high alert, but the question remains: Is the pilot a terrorist? Will he attempt to crash the plane he's currently flying?" The news was relentless, with varying theories and speculations. Sofia knew it was only a matter of time before military and CBI officials would storm the control room, turning the once serene environment into a high-stakes war room.

Meanwhile, Hoffs had just wrapped up his urgent conversation with Aury and was now faced with a critical decision. He decided to divide his team into two: one group, led by Lara and including Amelia, would search for Luna and the criminal, while the other half would investigate the blast site for additional clues.

Hoffs jumped into his modified Rubicon, the sleek black vehicle glinting under the sun. The growl of the 6.4L V8 engine roared to life, commanding attention as he sped off. "Where are you headed?" Lara shouted as Hoffs accelerated away, leaving a cloud of dust in his wake.

"To the airport to connect with Bill," Hoffs replied, shifting gears with determination. The Rubicon surged forward, quickly covering the ground.

The screech of brakes announced Hoffs's arrival at JFK Airport. He pulled up to the gate and flashed his ID card to the gatekeeper, who promptly lifted the barricade. Hoffs drove his Rubicon to the control tower parking lot, his vehicle occupying the space meant for two cars.

He leaped out of the vehicle, wincing slightly as he adjusted his shoulder—a reminder of the heavy door that had struck him during the blast. He called for the lift to the control tower, but the lift's slow progress prompted him to opt for the stairs.

It felt like an endless ascent, with each step and turn adding to his fatigue. By the time he reached the top, sweat poured down his face, and his shirt clung to his back as if he'd just stepped out of a shower.

Entering the control room, Hoffs found two young military personnel already on site. One was seated next to an air traffic controller, while the other stood nearby, their presence underscoring the seriousness of the situation. Hoffs approached them, his ID card held out for inspection.

"Officer Hoffs, New York CBI department," he introduced himself, his voice firm but tinged with exhaustion.

The military personnel exchanged a quick glance before one of them nodded. "We've been briefed about the situation. We're here to coordinate with you and ensure we handle this incident efficiently."

Sofia, observing the interaction from her station, felt the tension in the air shift as the room's atmosphere became charged with urgency. She was now on high alert, aware that the next few hours would be critical in resolving the crisis.

The control room, once a symbol of routine and order, was now at the epicenter of a high-stakes operation where every decision mattered.

# XIV
## Chapter 14

**The passengers, once relaxed and oblivious,**
began to shift uneasily in their seats. Their stomachs grumbled with hunger as the flight continued, now reaching the halfway point of its journey.

The usual hum of the aircraft was occasionally interrupted by murmurs of discomfort and frustration. Aury, aware of the mounting anxiety, faced a delicate situation. Although the meals were safe, the risk of water being tampered with had forced her to make a decision.

She approached Carie, who was already inspecting the juice stock. The array of colorful juice bottles glistened under the overhead lights, a welcome sight against the backdrop of their predicament. "We have more than enough juice to serve everyone," Carie confirmed, her voice tinged with a mix of reassurance and nervousness. "If anyone asks for water, we'll give them tap water in a glass."

Aury nodded. "Let's proceed with the food and juice service. We'll keep a close watch."

In the cabin, Aury's voice came over the intercom: "We apologize for the delay in our service. The inflight meal service will begin shortly." She and Jessica moved down the aisle, pushing the food trolley. John and Carie followed from the rear, carrying additional trays and supplies.

As they worked their way down the aisle, the contrast between the flight attendants' calm professionalism and the passengers' growing anxiety was evident. Despite the cheerful attempts to lighten the mood, the tension was palpable.

Meanwhile, Bill returned to the cockpit, where Leo was busy adjusting controls. "Costal zero-nine-four, maintaining altitude at thirty thousand feet with heading two-six-five towards west," Leo reported, his hands deftly maneuvering the dials. Bill settled into his seat, the headset back on, his mind racing with thoughts of Rafi and the potential danger onboard.

He glanced at his iPad, hoping for an update, but there was nothing new. The silence was abruptly broken by the arrival of a call. Bill's heart pounded as he accepted the call, and Rafi's face appeared on the screen, his surroundings shrouded in darkness. The dim light from the screen illuminated Rafi's face, casting an eerie glow against the black backdrop.

Bill wasted no time, typing quickly: "What did you do with Luna? How was that blast? Is she safe?"

Before Bill could finish, Rafi's voice cut through the static. "I see you're already informed. But let me assure you, your daughter is safe with me."

Rafi turned the camera, revealing Luna in a small, dimly lit compartment. The scene was grim: Luna sat on the cold metal floor, her hands bound. Her eyes were closed, and her body was still, making Bill's heart race with fear.

"Luna is just asleep," Rafi said, his tone dismissive. "A little injection to make her rest. She'll be awake soon."

Bill's fingers flew over the keyboard. "What did you do to her?" he typed frantically.

"Just a mild sedative," Rafi responded nonchalantly. "But that's not your concern right now. You know what's at stake. Choose between your passengers and your daughter."

The threat hung heavy in the air, and Bill's mind raced. "You're going to leave Luna alone?" he typed, his desperation clear.

Rafi's face twisted into a sly grin. "It's up to you. The passengers or your daughter—your choice."

The conversation took a darker turn. "About the blast, I knew you wouldn't stay idle. I anticipated your response. And now, Plan B."

"Plan B? What's that?" Bill's anxiety escalated.

"It's a surprise," Rafi replied, his smile widening. "A little twist to the game."

The call ended abruptly, leaving Bill reeling. His heart pounded as he pushed back in his chair, closing his eyes to regain composure. The weight of the situation pressed heavily on him—he couldn't bring himself to poison Leo, his closest friend, yet the alternative was unthinkable.

As he struggled to steady his breathing, he suddenly felt a cold, hard pressure against his temple. His eyes flew open to find an automatic pistol with a long silencer aimed directly at his head.

His pulse quickened, and a wave of dread washed over him. The silent threat was clear: if he didn't act swiftly, his own life and the lives of everyone on the flight could be at risk.

# XV
## Chapter 15

**Lara's SUV rumbled into the dark, deserted parking lot,**
its headlights cutting through the murky gloom. The lot was eerily quiet, save for the low hum of fluorescent lights flickering overhead. The entrance was cordoned off with bright yellow caution tape, the kind that flutters ominously in the wind.

A lone black car sat in the corner, its sinister presence accentuated by the dim lighting. On the opposite side, two military trucks loomed, their imposing silhouettes stark against the floodlit parking area. The reporters, huddled behind another stretch of caution tape, hovered anxiously, their cameras trained on the scene, waiting for any new developments.

Lara maneuvered the SUV to a stop and turned off the engine. Amelia, quick to act, flung open the door and leaped out, her movements swift and practiced.

Lara retrieved two helmets and a thick, tactical jacket from the back seat. She handed one of the jackets and helmets to Amelia, who donned them with a fluid motion. Lara adjusted her own helmet, its tinted visor reflecting the harsh lights of the parking lot.

"Stay behind the shield for now," Lara instructed, pointing towards a temporary room constructed from reinforced glass sheets. Amelia nodded and moved towards the temporary shelter, joining a colleague who was stationed there.

Lara advanced towards the black car, her eyes scanning the surroundings. The bomb squad was meticulously examining the vehicle. One of the technicians was using a thin metal probe to check for any hidden wires, while another slid under the car to inspect for explosive devices. A third technician worked on unlocking the car door, his tools clicking and clacking as he maneuvered them.

"We're running out of time," Lara muttered, glancing at the car's interior through the windows. The dashboard bore the crumpled remains of a tissue from an ice cream parlor—an insignificant detail, yet poignant in the context of the situation.

"Ma'am, please step back," one of the technicians urged. "We can't afford any mistakes. It's safer if you keep your distance."

Lara gave a curt nod and stepped back, her eyes never leaving the car. The tension in the parking lot was palpable. The technician finally managed to unlock the car door, his movements cautious and deliberate. The soft click of the door handle seemed to reverberate through the silent night.

Everyone held their breath as the technician slowly pulled the door open. The sudden gust of cold air that flowed out seemed almost surreal, and for a moment, the parking lot was frozen in anticipation.

Lara's hand instinctively went up to shield her face, her heart pounding in her chest. Amelia ducked under a table, and the others took defensive positions, bracing for any potential explosion.

Seconds ticked by like hours. The car's interior remained eerily calm, the quiet punctuated only by the distant sounds of reporters shouting and camera shutters clicking. The technician, still trembling, stepped out of the car and gave a relieved nod.

"There's nothing inside, ma'am. As you suspected, it's clean," he confirmed, his voice a mix of relief and exhaustion.

Lara exhaled slowly, her tension easing. She removed her helmet, running a hand through her damp hair. The oppressive heat of the parking lot seemed to dissipate, though the anxiety lingered. She turned and walked back to Amelia, who had just removed her jacket, wiping the sweat from her brow.

"Let's move," Lara said, her voice clipped but steady. "We need to find the next lead."

Amelia nodded, quickly buckling into the passenger seat as Lara slid into the driver's seat. Lara's hands gripped the wheel with purpose as she shifted the SUV into reverse. The tires screeched against the pavement as she maneuvered the vehicle away from the parking area.

Suddenly, Lara's radio crackled to life. "We've located the van. I repeat we've found the van." The message cut through the remaining tension like a knife.

Lara's eyes widened with renewed urgency. She slammed the gear into drive and sped towards the exit, her focus unwavering. Amelia fastened her seatbelt with a sense of grim determination, and the SUV roared to life, leaving the parking lot in a cloud of dust.

# XVI

## Chapter 16

**Luna's eyes fluttered open slowly,**
struggling to adjust to the dim light that seeped through the small air vent. The metallic interior around her was claustrophobic, a far cry from the spacious world she was used to. Her hands were tightly bound with the rope that had been taken from their garden, but her body was free. She tried to recall the events leading up to this moment: the last thing she remembered was sitting in the chair, tears streaming down her face, and then a sharp prick in her shoulder from a small injection.

The compartment was cramped, with just enough space for her to sit or lie down, but barely room to stand. The temperature was sweltering, and the tiny gusts of air from the vent felt like a godsend. Luna's initial fear of being packed into a container for shipment began to dissipate as she took in her surroundings. She soon realized she was inside the service van that had come to their house to repair the telephone.

The compartment door creaked open with a loud metallic groan. Luna's eyes squinted against the sudden burst of light, revealing a narrow alleyway outside. The street was flanked by large trash bins, their presence adding to the griminess of the alley. Above, a noisy exhaust fan churned, its hum filling the silence. A pair of vending machines stood forlornly in the distance, coated in grime, suggesting they hadn't seen much use in a long time.

The temperature inside the compartment dropped slightly as the door remained open. Rafi entered, holding a small, chilled bottle of water. He tossed it to Luna, who struggled to open the cap with her tied hands. Noticing her difficulty, Rafi unscrewed it for her and handed it back. Luna drank eagerly, the cool liquid offering a brief respite from her thirst.

As she finished, Rafi settled into a corner near the door, his presence looming. Luna took a deep breath and broke the silence. "You told me your name is Rafi. Why did you kidnap me?"

Rafi took a sip of his cola and crushed the can with a satisfying crunch. "Because your father is piloting a target plane today."

"Target plane?" Luna's voice wavered with confusion. "What do you mean?"

Rafi's eyes glinted with a chilling resolve. "We're going to crash that plane."

The revelation hit Luna like a punch to the gut. She struggled to contain her shock, her mind racing. "You mean you're going to blow it up?"

"No," Rafi corrected with a grim smile. "We're going to crash it. Our mission is to create a catastrophe."

Luna's face paled. "Is it going to be like 9/11?"

Rafi's chest swelled with pride as he nodded. "Probably bigger."

"Which terrorist group do you belong to?" Luna asked, her voice trembling.

Rafi shook his head. "We don't belong to any group. We're independent. Just me and my brother."

He walked over to one of the vending machines and inserted some coins. The machine whirred, and a chocolate bar clunked down. Rafi retrieved it and approached Luna, holding it out. "Here, have this. You might be hungry."

Luna eyed the chocolate warily. "There's nothing in it?" she asked, her voice barely a whisper.

"Nothing harmful," Rafi assured. "It's just to keep you from falling asleep again. You're not going to die from it."

Meanwhile, back on the plane, Aury was busy collecting the last of the food trays. She handed a chocolate bar to a passenger as a complimentary dessert, apologizing for the delay. The mood in the cabin had been relatively calm, with passengers enjoying their meals, watching movies, or chatting with one another.

As Aury maneuvered the trolley back to its place, she noticed John still attending to a few passengers at the rear of the plane, while Jessica finished serving the final dessert in business class. Aury took a seat on a jump seat, removing her gloves and tossing them into the trash. She pulled out her phone, hoping for an update from Hoffs or Amelia, but found none.

Just then, a notification popped up on her screen: ***"TERRORIST FLYING FLIGHT 094, ONE BLAST IN THE CITY. NOW IT MIGHT BE THE PLANE."***

Aury's heart skipped a beat as she read the headline. She wasn't the only one who saw it; the news spread quickly among the passengers. Initial confusion gave way to growing fear as they realized the gravity of the situation—they were on the same flight. The tension in the cabin mounted rapidly. Flight attendant call buttons started to blink incessantly as passengers, now visibly distressed, sought help.

Aury's face went pale. She quickly gathered her composure and sprang into action, her mind racing through the procedures for such an emergency. She needed to reassure the passengers and maintain control of the situation while trying to find out what was happening. The stakes were higher than ever, and she knew every second counted.

# XVII

## Chapter 17

**Bill's heart pounded in his chest as he instinctively raised his hands in a defensive gesture.**

The cockpit fell into an eerie silence, the constant hum of the jet engines outside the only sound piercing the tense atmosphere. As Bill turned his head slowly to the right, he saw Leo standing there, a cold and calculated expression on his face. The shock was immediate and profound—his best friend was holding the gun.

"What are you doing, Leo?" Bill's voice was strained, a mix of confusion and disbelief. Leo's response was chilling. He pushed a button in front of him, severing their audio connection with the control tower. The radio went silent, leaving Bill alone with his thoughts and fears.

Bill's mind raced as he processed the situation. His gaze locked onto the new message that had popped up on his iPad: "Meet my brother Leo." The words hung ominously in the air as if mocking his desperation for answers.

"What does that mean?" Bill demanded, his voice barely concealing his turmoil.

"I'm with Rafi," Leo said coldly. "And I'm going to help him take down the plane."

Bill's heart sank as he struggled to comprehend Leo's betrayal. "I don't believe this. Did Rafi even kidnap someone from your family?"

"No," Leo replied flatly.

Bill's confusion deepened. "What do you mean by 'no'? If you're with Rafi, then why—"

Leo cut him off, turning his gaze to the window. "Whatever is happening was my plan from the start."

Bill's face twisted in disbelief. "Yes, it is true, and Rafi is my brother."

The revelation was a gut punch to Bill. Leo, his closest friend, was the mastermind behind this nightmare, and he was working with Rafi, the very person responsible for Luna's abduction.

"So, you're saying you're behind this plan. But why, Leo?" Bill's voice wavered with a mix of anger and hurt. "Why are you doing this? Why do you want to crash the plane and kill all of us?"

Leo's head drooped as he stared blankly at the cockpit table. His silence spoke volumes, revealing the depth of his resolve or perhaps his inner conflict. "That's none of your business. You just have to follow through and crash the plane."

Bill's face flushed with frustration. "So this was your Plan B? I never expected this from you. You're not the Leo I know. You're not the person who was Luna's favorite uncle."

Leo's eyes flickered with something—regret, maybe, but it was fleeting. "Just do what you're told," Leo shouted, his voice sharp and unyielding.

Bill's anger boiled over. "I should have mixed that powder into your tea. At least I would have been alone in the cockpit."

Leo's lips curled into a sardonic smile. "The powder? That was just sugar."

"But Rafi said it would put you to sleep," Bill countered, his voice trembling.

"If you'd mixed it, I would have just pretended to sleep," Leo said dismissively. "In the end, I have to make sure you crash the plane."

The casual way Leo spoke about such a grave matter only deepened Bill's despair. He slumped back in his seat, closing his eyes and trying to suppress the wave of emotions crashing over him. This betrayal was a wound that cut deeper than any physical injury.

Leo had been his confidant, his partner in countless missions, and the person who had been a rock in his life. To learn that Leo was behind such a horrific plot, orchestrating it from the shadows, was almost too much to bear.

Leo's hand reached for the button again, and the radio crackled back to life. "Coastal Zero-Nine-Four, it seems there are some weather issues with the radio. Continue maintaining thirty thousand feet altitude."

Bill's heart sank further. The calm, almost casual tone Leo used belied the gravity of their situation. Leo's laughter, tinged with a dark amusement, echoed through the cockpit. "They must deserve an Oscar for their acting. They sent the FBI to your house, and now they're scouring the city for Luna. We're all over the news. And yet, they try to act as if nothing's wrong. Really great actors out there."

Bill's stomach churned as he processed the magnitude of their deception. The facade of normalcy they maintained was a twisted play, hiding the real horror from the world.

# XVIII
## Chapter 18

**Leo and Rafi sprinted through the narrow alley,**
their bare feet slapping against the hot, uneven pavement. The sweltering heat of the summer evening was relentless, and sweat streamed down their faces as they darted past pedestrians and dodged obstacles.

Leo's breath came in ragged gasps, and he wiped his forehead with the back of his hand, determined to keep moving. Rafi, equally drenched, followed closely, their pace a frantic blur of movement and adrenaline.

As they approached a high clay wall, Leo leaped over it with ease, and Rafi followed in his wake, barely managing to clear the top. They landed on the other side, sending up a splash of dust that hung in the air like a shroud.

The two boys kept running, their shorts and t-shirts sticking to their sweat-soaked skin. They stumbled over puddles and each other, but their shared goal kept them going. Their relentless pace was not just a race, but a synchronized effort to escape their everyday struggles and chase a fleeting dream.

Eventually, Leo skidded to a stop in front of a bustling café. His chest heaved as he caught his breath, and Rafi arrived a moment later, equally winded. They exchanged quick, determined glances before plunging into the crowded café.

The interior was thick with smoke and loud with the clamor of animated conversations and clinking glasses. The air was charged with the heady mix of cigarette smoke and the aroma of strong coffee and alcohol.

Navigating through the haze, they made their way to the reception desk. The lady behind it engulfed in a cloud of smoke, glanced up from her position with a weary expression. Leo, with a swift motion, pulled a handful of coins from his pocket and placed them on the table.

The woman examined the coins with a practiced eye, counting them meticulously. She paused momentarily, her gaze flicking between the boys and the coins, before sliding them into a drawer and extracting two shiny tokens, which she placed on the counter.

Without a word, Leo snatched the tokens and tucked them into his pocket. The woman, struggling with her bulky frame, slowly got up from her chair. She lumbered to a door at the side of the reception area and opened it, revealing a darkened room beyond. Leo and Rafi rushed through the door, their footsteps echoing as they navigated the dimly lit hallway.

Inside, the room was shrouded in darkness, save for the light filtering through the cracks of the closed door. They clambered up a steep flight of stairs, elbowing past a few patrons who had already settled in their seats. At the top, they reached a wide, open space with a large white curtain stretched across one wall. They plopped down on the lowest tier of the makeshift seating area, their excitement palpable.

The room fell into a hush as a buzzer sounded, signaling the beginning of the show. A beam of light pierced through the darkness, illuminating the curtain and casting a glow across the audience. Slowly, images began to appear, and the anticipation in the air grew electric. The words "TOP GUN" flashed across the screen, and the crowd erupted in cheers.

For the next two hours, the world outside ceased to exist. The boys were entranced by the vibrant spectacle unfolding before them. The screen came alive with images of sun-drenched beaches, sleek motorcycles, and glamorous women.

Men in military uniforms, aviation sunglasses, and state-of-the-art aircraft soared through the sky, captivating Leo and Rafi with their every maneuver. The movie's fast-paced action and charismatic characters held them in a spellbound trance. The experience was nothing short of a revelation, painting a picture of a life they had only dared to dream about.

As the final credits rolled and the screen faded to black, the café's patrons began to disperse. Laughter and conversation filled the air as people exited, but Leo and Rafi remained seated, their eyes fixed on the now-dark screen.

The profound impact of what they had just witnessed was evident in their expressions. They exchanged a glance, a silent understanding passing between them. Words seemed unnecessary; the shared experience had spoken volumes.

When the room was finally empty, Leo and Rafi emerged, their minds buzzing with new resolve. The next morning, the two friends sat down with a renewed sense of purpose. They began to map out their future with a determination that had been ignited by their cinematic journey.

They would save every penny they could, start learning English, and one day, make their way to America.

# XIX

## Chapter 19

**The cabin was a maelstrom of confusion and fear.**

The news of the potential terrorist threat had ignited widespread panic. Amidst the chaos, a young man's desperate cry pierced the clamor, "We all are going to die!" His words, charged with raw fear, echoed through the cabin, amplifying the already palpable anxiety.

John, acting swiftly, rushed towards the source of the commotion and clamped his hands over the man's mouth, pulling him back with a firm grip. Despite his efforts, the cabin's atmosphere grew even more chaotic, as panic and dread rippled through the passengers.

Aury's heart raced as she saw the situation spiraling out of control. The din of terrified voices and the shrieks of alarmed passengers made it almost impossible to hear her thoughts. She knew that if the panic escalated further, it would lead to a stampede for the limited water supplies, which could exacerbate the crisis. With a quick decision, she grabbed the handset of the intercom, her voice trembling but resolute as she spoke into it.

"Ladies and gentlemen, we request you to please be seated and remain calm. We are here to ensure your safety and are doing everything in our power to manage the situation."

Her words, though intended to soothe, were barely audible over the cacophony of fear and shouting. The other crew members, having already begun to navigate through the aisle to calm the passengers, struggled to restore some semblance of order.

John, meanwhile, had managed to contain the young man who had instigated the commotion. He guided him to a jump seat, his eyes scanning the man for any hidden weapons or dangerous objects. To his relief, he found none and released him after a thorough check.

"What's the meaning of this? Why did you drag me up here?" the young man protested, his voice laced with confusion and fear.

John, trying to defuse the tension, handed him a glass of orange juice. "I'm really sorry for the misunderstanding, sir. We thought you might be involved in something else. Here, have some juice. Try to calm down."

The man took the juice, his hands still shaking. He took a long sip, visibly relieved by the cold liquid, though his eyes remained wide with fear. "I'm not one of them, but the pilot is," he said, his voice quivering.

John's laugh was short and nervous. "Don't take everything you hear seriously. It's just sensationalism. They're trying to scare people."

As he escorted the man back to his seat, the situation in the cabin began to stabilize slightly. The chaos subsided, though the anxiety remained. Passengers continued to murmur among themselves, weaving their own theories and speculations. Some stories were optimistic, while others only deepened the sense of dread.

Aury, still troubled by the situation, decided it was time to address the passengers directly again. She walked back to the front of the plane, her movements purposeful despite the turmoil. Gripping the mic firmly, she took a deep breath before speaking.

"Ladies and gentlemen, I know the information you've received is alarming, and I want to clarify a few things. The situation we are facing is serious, but there are some crucial points to understand."

The cabin fell into an uneasy silence as passengers strained to hear her over the low hum of the plane's engines.

"Firstly, yes, there was indeed a bomb blast at Captain Bill's house. However, Captain Bill himself is not a terrorist. His daughter, Luna, has been kidnapped by a group of individuals who are demanding that he crash this plane to save her."

A collective gasp echoed through the cabin, and panic surged again as the gravity of her words set in. The fear was almost tangible, but Aury pressed on, her voice steady.

"While it is true that Captain Bill is under tremendous pressure and the situation is critical, we have the FBI and military working tirelessly to locate and rescue Luna. We must not lose hope. Although you may be worried, it's important to remain calm and not exacerbate the situation."

The fear in the cabin was palpable, but Aury's words seemed to offer a glimmer of reassurance. "For now, the best thing we can do is to stay calm and follow instructions. The crew and authorities are doing everything they can to ensure your safety. Please pray for a positive outcome and trust that we are working hard to resolve this situation."

As she finished, Aury offered a small, encouraging smile. The murmur of conversations resumed, but the atmosphere had shifted slightly. The passengers appeared more composed, their fears tempered by a renewed sense of hope.

Although anxiety still lingered, the cabin was now filled with a quieter, more hopeful murmur. Aury took a deep breath, her nerves frayed but her resolve firm. She knew that staying calm and collected was crucial, both for the passengers and for herself, as they navigated through this perilous situation.

# XX

# Chapter 20

**"Flight nine-one-two, clear for take-off,"**

Sofia announced through the mic, her voice steady as she pressed the green button on her desk. With a sigh of relief, she sank back into her chair. "This is the last flight for the night. Most flights have been redirected to safer airspace," she added, glancing at Hoffs, who was absorbed in the files and records of the pilots from Flight 094.

Hoffs slammed the files down onto the table beside him, his frustration evident. "Nothing," he muttered, shaking his head in exasperation.

Hud, leaning back and smoking a cigarette, looked up with a mixture of disbelief and resignation. "We've told you before. Both pilots are ex-Air Force, and highly trained. It's hard to believe they'd be involved in something like this."

Hoffs, clearly agitated, pounded his fist against the wall. "I know... I know..." Hud's voice was calm but tinged with irritation as he tossed his cigarette aside.

"I've worked with both of them," Hud continued his tone firm. "They were known for their exceptional skills and their tight-knit friendship. It's almost inconceivable they'd be behind this."

Ignoring Hud's reassurance, Hoffs grabbed the file again, flipping through it with increasing frustration. "We need to find the girl and the kidnappers," Hud said, stirring his coffee as he watched Hoffs' growing agitation. "My team is already on it."

Hud's dismissive attitude towards the kidnapping seemed to fuel Hoffs' anger. "You think that girl is just a pawn in this? Do you really think that by merely looking at her the kidnapper will surrender?"

The other military man chuckled, joining in on the dark humor of the situation. Hud smirked, taking another sip of his coffee, seemingly indifferent to the seriousness of the situation.

In a sudden outburst, Hoffs threw the file aside and stormed towards Hud. The tension in the room spiked as Hoffs pulled out his gun, aiming it at Hud's head. He grabbed Hud by the collar, his face flushed with anger. "Dare you to say another word about her," he growled, his voice low and dangerous.

The room erupted into chaos. Everyone's eyes were on the confrontation, the atmosphere thick with tension. Hud, unflustered, calmly pushed the gun away, his expression unreadable. In an instant, he used his quick reflexes to disable Hoffs. With a swift motion, Hud pressed one of his fingers into Hoffs's ribs, a technique that paralyzed him momentarily. Hoffs dropped to the ground, groaning in pain.

Hud straightened his uniform with a practiced flick, wiping away coffee stains with a tissue. As he made his way back to the coffee machine, Hoffs struggled to get back on his feet, his anger still simmering. Sofia, shocked by the sudden outburst, shouted, "Stop!"

The room fell into a heavy silence as Hoffs' fist hovered dangerously close to Hud's head. The entire room seemed to hold its breath, waiting for the next move. Finally, Hoffs bolstered his gun, his face a mask of barely controlled rage. He returned to his seat, while Hud resumed his coffee-making with an air of casual indifference.

Sofia, shaken but resolute, returned to her desk. She adjusted her headset, refocusing on her tasks. As she filled out some paperwork, her attention was abruptly drawn to a peculiar sound emanating from the headset. She pressed the cuffs tighter to her ears, her brow furrowing in concentration.

Noticing Sofia's distress, Hud approached her. "What's going on?" he asked, taking another sip of his coffee, his curiosity piqued.

"There's a strange noise coming from Flight 094," Sofia said, her voice laced with concern. "It sounds like a clicking sound."

Hud's expression shifted as he took the headset from Sofia and listened intently. His eyes widened in recognition. "Damn… it's Morse code," he said, his voice tinged with urgency.

Without wasting a moment, Hud grabbed a sheet of paper from a nearby shelf and snatched a pen from Sofia's hand. He sat down at her desk and began to decode the Morse code, his movements precise and focused. Each tap and dot was translated into critical information, his mind racing as he worked to unravel the message hidden in the coded signals.

# XXI
## Chapter 21

**The brakes of Lara's car screeched as she brought the vehicle to a halt in front of the alleyway.**

They were the first to arrive at the scene, and the stark difference from the chaotic frenzy earlier was palpable. The area was unusually quiet, lacking the bomb squad, media frenzy, and flashing cameras that had previously characterized it.

This time, the only activity was a small group of men loitering near a wall, their vague silhouettes obscured by the dim light of the alley. They appeared to be engaged in smoking, though the substance was unclear. Amelia tried to avert her gaze from them, her expression one of mild distaste, while Lara, more focused and determined, paid little attention to their presence. As the men noticed Lara's car, they shuffled away, retreating to a shadowy corner.

Amelia quickly exited the vehicle, her movements cautious as she kicked a few stray cans out of her path. The alley was littered with garbage and the stench was overpowering. She stepped gingerly, trying to avoid the detritus on the ground. A drop of water fell onto her face from a leaking AC vent above, causing her to shiver involuntarily. She wiped her face and quickened her pace to keep up with Lara.

In the middle of the alley, Lara halted and reached into her jeans, pulling out a gun and tossing it towards Amelia. Amelia caught it with a swift, practiced motion, her eyes scanning the weapon. "Keep this for your safety," Lara instructed, her voice steady and no-nonsense. "I hope you know how to use it."

"Of course, it's America," Amelia replied, her voice tinged with a hint of bravado as she examined the magazine and the bullets.

Lara's eyes narrowed slightly as she warned, "Use it only in case of emergency."

Amelia nodded, carefully reloading the magazine and tucking the gun into her jeans, ensuring it was covered by her top. They continued forward, moving cautiously towards the end of the alley. As they approached the van, Lara took cover behind a trash bin, her posture alert. Amelia positioned herself behind a nearby vending machine, the odd assortment of snacks inside seeming almost foreign to her.

Lara signaled Amelia to stay put, but Amelia's curiosity got the better of her. She followed Lara as they edged closer to the van, taking cover behind various obstacles along the way. Lara's movements were deliberate and controlled; she had her gun drawn and ready, its top slid back for a quick load if needed.

They finally reached the van. Lara took cover behind it, while Amelia remained a few steps behind, peering cautiously from behind the vending machine. Her heart raced as she saw Lara crouch near the driver's door, carefully peeking inside. Finding the cab empty, Lara pushed the door open, revealing an unremarkable interior.

Lara moved to the back of the van, her movements steady and deliberate. She grabbed the handle of the back door, her breath catching as she prepared for the worst. Amelia closed her eyes, bracing herself for any potential danger. With a metallic creak, the door swung open, and Amelia peeked through the gap. The interior was just as empty as the front—filled only with a few telephone cables and tools scattered in one corner.

Amelia gingerly stepped into the compartment, her smartphone flashlight cutting through the dimness. She scanned the space for any clues or hidden items but found nothing of significance. The tension of their search seemed to dissipate slightly as they completed their inspection.

Before long, other members of the police department and FBI agents arrived, swiftly securing the area. Their presence brought a renewed sense of urgency and control to the scene. The media, ever eager for a story, followed closely behind, their cameras and microphones creating a new wave of activity and noise.

The once-quiet alleyway transformed into a bustling hub of activity. The press huddled near the edge of the scene, their flashing cameras capturing every moment as law enforcement officials coordinated their efforts. The chaos of the media contrasted sharply with the earlier calm, emphasizing the gravity of the situation as the search for Luna and the terrorists continued.

# XXII
## Chapter 22

**Bill's iPad vibrated insistently on the table in front of him.**

The persistent buzzing was almost as loud as the roar of the jet engines outside. He kept his eyes closed, trying to drown out the chaos around him. With a weary sigh, he reached for the iPad, pulling out his headset and setting it aside. He plugged in his earphones, the familiar click of the connector doing little to ease his mounting tension.

Finally, he picked up the iPad, bracing himself for what was to come. The screen flickered to life, revealing the same face he had seen before. This time, however, the view was different. The man appeared to be driving an old-fashioned car, the dashboard and interior looking vintage and out of place. The phone was mounted on a bracket next to him, offering a stable view.

"So, we are soon reaching our destination," the man said with a smirk, his voice carrying a note of satisfaction. Bill's frustration was palpable, but he remained silent, choosing to conserve his energy for the critical moments ahead.

The man's demeanor shifted slightly as he added, "You want to see your daughter, don't you?" The mere mention of Luna's name sent a surge of adrenaline through Bill. He leaned closer to the screen, his gaze locked onto the image of his daughter.

The man turned the camera to the back seat, where Luna was sitting, her hands still bound and her mouth sealed. She was awake now, her eyes filled with a mixture of fear and resignation. Bill and Luna exchanged a silent, poignant look, communicating through their eyes as if to say everything they could not with words.

The man turned the phone back to himself, glancing at his watch. "Exactly two hours," he said with a dark satisfaction. Bill's heart sank as he watched Leo in the cockpit, his expression unreadable as he turned off the radio.

"Enough of the acting," the man said, his voice cold and detached. Bill's anxiety was palpable as he glanced at Leo, who now wore a smirk. Leo was clearly part of the plan, a fact that Bill found hard to accept.

The man continued, "Leo is there to help you while you're crashing the plane. Making it easier—no one's going to disturb you." As he spoke, Leo reached over and pushed a button beside Bill, locking the door behind him with an audible click.

"There would hardly be any chaos during the crash," the man said, his tone almost clinical. "What do you mean?" Bill's voice trembled with dread. "In simple terms," the man explained, "all your passengers will be dead before the crash happens."

Bill's eyes widened in shock. "What?" he choked out, his voice barely a whisper.

The man's voice grew more sinister. "It's like flying a huge coffin directly to the graveyard. For you, it's the Times Square." The gravity of the situation was unbearable. "How would you kill them?" Bill asked, his voice cracking under the pressure.

"Simple," the man replied. "Leo is going to decompress the cabin slowly. By the time they realize what's happening, they'll be dead. The oxygen masks will drop automatically, but breathing the oxygen from them will actually kill them faster."

Bill was confused and horrified. "How can something meant to save lives cause death?" he questioned.

The man's response was chilling. "The oxygen masks will cause rapid decompression, accelerating their demise. From now on, Leo will guide you and help you out. And remember," he said, showing a red button encased in a glass box, "if anything goes wrong, I'll just press this and... boom." He turned the camera towards Luna. "No!" Bill screamed; his voice filled with desperation as the call abruptly ended.

The cockpit fell into an eerie silence. Leo leaned forward, adjusting a dial slightly before pressing a button. A green light next to it illuminated, signaling that they were back on the radio. Leo spoke into his mic, "Coastal flight zero-nine-four, facing issues with connectivity. Maintaining altitude thirty thousand feet, heading two-seven-one west."

A reply came swiftly from the other side, acknowledging the transmission. Bill's gaze shifted towards Leo, his expression a mix of anger and resignation. Leo's actions were unmistakable—he was slowly decompressing the cabin; a fact Bill knew all too well.

With a sense of urgency, Bill moved his hand subtly, placing his fingers on his mic. He attempted to transmit Morse code, his hope hanging on whether anyone on the ground would recognize the signal. His heart raced as he fought to maintain composure, knowing that this was his last, desperate attempt to communicate and perhaps prevent the impending catastrophe.

# XXIII
## Chapter 23

**Hud sat at the desk, headset clamped to one ear**, waiting for any sign of a message. The silence was deafening, only interrupted by the occasional beep from the speakers. His patience was wearing thin. Sofia sat next to him, juggling multiple screens and directing the diversion of other flights. Hoffs leaned against a nearby wall, engrossed in files and records, his frustration evident.

"Did you get anything?" Sofia asked, glancing at Hud with a mix of hope and impatience.

"Negative," Hud responded in a gravelly voice, lighting a cigar. The smoke curled lazily into the air. He took a long drag, his eyes never leaving the array of screens in front of him.

Sofia, clearly agitated, turned her attention to Hoffs. "Nothing yet?"

Hoffs shook his head, exasperated. "How would he even know we can hear him?"

"Exactly," Sofia added, moving closer to Hud. "Why don't we just let him know that we can hear him?"

"Don't be so reckless," Sofia retorted, her frustration palpable. "Both pilots can hear us, and we don't even know if the other pilot is aware of the hijacking. Announcing our presence might only complicate things further."

Hud pulled out a wireless communicator from his jacket and began pressing buttons. "Prepare four F-16s," he instructed, his tone nonchalant.

Sofia's eyes widened in disbelief. "Are you serious? You want to take down the plane?"

Hud chuckled. "Not really. I know Bill. He won't let us do that. It's just for formalities." His casual demeanor contrasted sharply with the gravity of the situation.

The speaker crackled, and everyone went silent, their attention snapping back to the screens. Hud pressed his cigar between his teeth and adjusted the cuffs of his headset. He clicked his pen, and the rhythmic scratching of paper filled the room as he began to decode a new message.

"The cabin is being slowly decompressed," Hud read aloud as he scribbled down notes. "Do not let the passengers use the oxygen masks. I repeat, do not use the oxygen masks. They will kill them in seconds. That's all I know."

Sofia read over his shoulder, her expression one of deep concern. "Has he gone mad? He's saying the cabin will be decompressed but warns against using the oxygen masks?"

Hoffs looked equally bewildered. "It doesn't make sense."

Hud's demeanor remained calm as he shuffled through papers on his desk. "We need to act quickly. Tell Aury to seal every oxygen mask immediately. We don't have much time."

Hoffs pulled out his phone and began typing a message to Aury, but then paused, glancing at Hud. "How did you know I was in contact with the cabin? I don't think I ever mentioned it."

Hud's lips curled into a wry smile. "Do your job, child."

Hoffs shook his head, still perplexed, and resumed typing out the urgent message. He continued to narrate the situation to Aury, his frustration growing with each passing second.

Hud returned to his desk, papers spread out before him. Hoffs followed him, eyes fixed on the documents. One paper had a picture of Leo, the first officer, while another showed a different man. Additional papers contained records and notes.

"See, the plane went for service just before this flight," Hud explained, pointing to the records. "Everything was normal and fine during the service."

Hoffs, still standing on the other side of the table, looked at the records. "That's what they said."

Hud ignored the comment and continued, "This is Rafi, the service technician in charge." Hoffs pulled out his phone to contact Rafi but paused as Hud continued. "And this is our first officer, Leo."

Sofia leaned in, examining the papers. "So what's the connection?"

"Interestingly, they're brothers," Hud said, his voice carrying a note of grim satisfaction.

Hoffs looked at the papers, his eyes widening. "How are they connected?"

Hud picked up another sheet, revealing detailed records. "The chemical tanks that provide oxygen were replaced during the last service."

Sofia frowned, scanning the paper. "They were expired."

"Exactly," Hud replied. "But this plane is new, less than two years old. These components shouldn't have expired so soon."

The room fell into a contemplative silence.

Hud continued, "Here's a twist. Both brothers come from a poor family in the Middle East. They migrated here with dreams of becoming pilots. Their entire village was wiped out in a war, though they were innocent."

Sofia and Hoffs exchanged glances, the pieces of the puzzle slowly falling into place.

Hud's tone grew somber. "The first officer seems to be the victim here. And the kidnapper might very well be his brother."

Hoffs's face darkened with anger. "So, the brother is the one behind this?"

"Not entirely sure," Hud admitted. "But it's a possibility. We need to act fast and figure this out before it's too late."

# XXIV

## Chapter 24

**Aury finally settled into her jump seat after the cabin had calmed down a bit.**

She knew the peace was fragile and wouldn't last long. Some passengers were still crying out for help while others clung to their faith, whispering desperate prayers for their lives. The atmosphere was tense, with a mixture of panic and resignation hanging in the air.

Most of the passengers were trying to cooperate, but a few were demanding to enter the cockpit or speak with the pilots, convinced that a direct conversation would lead to a safe landing. The cockpit door remained firmly locked, and Aury could only hope that the situation up front was under control.

She peered through the small window on the door, gazing out at the clear sky and scattered clouds. The view was eerily familiar, reminding her of countless flights along this route.

Aury reached for her phone, which was buried in her handbag. As she turned it on, a flood of notifications from Hoffs lit up the screen. Her face paled as she read through the messages, her expressions shifting from confusion to fear. She quickly moved to the intercom, pressing the button to broadcast an urgent announcement.

The chirp of the intercom echoed through the cabin, making some passengers jump. John, who was seated at the back, immediately jumped up, rushing to Aury's side. The sound of his footsteps made the cabin's anxiety spike further. Passengers' fears turned into wild speculation about the imminent crash and accusations about the crew's loyalty.

"What's happening now?" John asked, his voice tight with worry.

"They're going to decompress the cabin, and there's poison in the oxygen masks," Aury said, her voice trembling.

John's face turned ashen. "Shit. How are we supposed to save the passengers in a decompressed cabin without oxygen masks? It's impossible."

Aury moved quickly to a nearby shelf, opening the top cupboard and pulling out a few oxygen masks and cylinders. She laid them out on the floor, her hands shaking. "We have six masks here," she said, glancing at John.

"There should be six more at the back," John added. "But that's still not enough for everyone. We have children and elderly passengers on board. Who do we give them to?"

Aury paced back and forth, her anxiety palpable. "What can we do now?"

John's mind raced as he tried to come up with a plan. "So, you said the cabin will decompress slowly?"

"Yes," Aury replied. "But why? If they want to kill us, why not do it instantly?"

Aury's face was a mix of fear and determination. "Maybe they want to kill us with the poison. The gradual decompression would make the oxygen masks drop down automatically. In panic, people will grab them and the poisonous gas will spread throughout the cabin."

John's face turned pale as he shivered at the thought. "We need to stop the oxygen masks from deploying. If we don't, the poison will spread even if the masks don't drop."

Aury's eyes darted to a drawer, where she pulled out a stack of zip locks. "We need to seal off the oxygen mask supply pipes manually. We can't let the masks drop."

John nodded, already calling the other crew members to the galley. They gathered around as Aury quickly briefed them on the situation. She explained the urgency and the plan: to manually pull down each oxygen mask and seal the supply pipes with the zip locks.

The crew members nodded in agreement, and soon volunteers began to step forward. Two men from the business class raised their hands, eager to help. A lady from the front row of the economy class also offered her assistance. Within moments, they had gathered a team of ten volunteers.

Aury felt a flicker of relief, though her anxiety lingered. She had been wary of one of the men, who had a deep scar running from his forehead to his nose. His appearance had initially made her uneasy. But as she got to know him, she discovered he was kind-hearted and had a good sense of humor. The scar, he explained, was from a recent accident, and he had been trying to lighten the mood with his jokes.

With the team assembled, Aury quickly briefed them on their tasks. She demonstrated how to pull down the masks manually, showing them the technique using a spare mask from the emergency briefing kit. John supervised the distribution of the zip locks, assigning each volunteer a specific section of the plane to cover.

The volunteers moved to their assigned positions, each one carrying out their duties with determination. They worked quickly and efficiently, sealing off the oxygen masks and ensuring that the poisonous gas would not be released into the cabin.

As the team worked, Aury watched from the galley, her heart pounding with every passing second. The cabin's atmosphere remained tense, but the volunteers' efforts were making a difference. The hope of saving the passengers was a beacon in the dark, and Aury clung to it as she watched the progress unfold.

# Chapter 25

**The car finally came to a halt in the empty parking lot near East River State Park.**

It was mid-afternoon, and the scorching heat had deterred most people from venturing out. Rafi stepped out first, grabbing a coat from the back seat.

The car groaned in protest as the door opened, its old age evident in every creak and rattle. Inside, Luna shifted uncomfortably, struggling to maneuver her bound hands as she tried to exit. The car, a worn-out relic from decades past, vibrated ominously when the engine was running as if every part were fighting to keep the vehicle alive.

Rafi pulled Luna out, roughly removing the tape from her mouth. She gasped, breathing deeply as the adhesive released her lips. The sensation of air on her dry mouth was a small relief. He draped the coat around her shoulders to conceal the intricate network of wires and the small chip attached to her chest. Her hands were still tied in front of her, but Rafi had done his best to hide the explosive strapped to her body.

As they entered the park, Rafi walked ahead, shielding Luna's bound hands from any onlookers. Not that there were many—on such a sweltering day, the park was almost deserted. After a short, tense walk, he led her to a bench shaded by an old oak tree, its leaves rustling faintly in the faint breeze.

Luna sat silently, her eyes drifting to familiar corners of the park. Memories washed over her, pulling her back to the days when this place had been her sanctuary.

"Ollie, stop running!" Luna's voice echoed in her head, and the memory of her childhood dog, a boisterous Labrador, came alive in her mind. She used to chase him across the park, the leash slipping from her hands as Ollie darted playfully through the grass. Her dad followed behind, laughing at her futile attempts to catch him. Every day, without fail, they visited the park—mornings filled with golden sunlight, and evenings spent watching the sunset over the river.

The park had been their playground, a haven where they could escape life's troubles. During the summers, they would play fetch under the blazing sun, Ollie bounding after the ball with relentless energy. In the autumn, they'd crunch through leaves, the crisp air filling their lungs.

Sometimes, they didn't even need to do much—just running wild together, laughing until they were exhausted. And when her father was too tired to keep up, he would sit on the very bench Luna now occupied, watching her with a contented smile. The ice cream parlor by the river was always their last stop—Luna loved dragging her dad to buy her a cone before they sat on the grass, the river glittering as the day faded to dusk.

Ollie, her loyal shadow, was always by her side. Even at home, the dog followed her around—through the house, to school, and finally to bed, where he would curl up beside her, chasing away any loneliness she might feel in the absence of her mother. For years, Ollie was the constant presence that filled the gaps in her heart.

But things changed. As Luna grew older, school, friends, and other responsibilities began to take her away from the park and Ollie. They didn't visit as often, and it was her dad who took over walking Ollie, strolling through their neighborhood instead of the sprawling park they once loved. Life had shifted in subtle ways, and Ollie grew older too.

The day Ollie didn't wake up was one of the worst in Luna's life. She remembered sitting beside her beloved companion, her small hands resting on his fur, tears streaming down her face. She refused to leave his side, even though her dad gently explained that Ollie had gone.

The vet confirmed it. Ollie wouldn't wake up again. That day, they made the difficult decision to bury him in the park, where he had been happiest. Her father dug the grave near their favorite bench, and Luna, with trembling hands, laid Ollie to rest. They covered him with soil, and Luna placed a small bouquet on the fresh mound. Her father placed a simple marble plaque beside it, etched with Ollie's name and age.

They visited often at first, every weekend, cleaning the spot and sitting together in silent remembrance. But the visits grew less frequent, and soon, a year had passed since Luna had last been in the park. Now, sitting there again, the memories of those times weighed heavily on her.

Rafi was engrossed in his phone, his fingers tapping away as if the weight of what they were about to do didn't affect him. Luna glanced around, taking in how much the park had changed. The ice cream parlor had been replaced by a hot dog stand. Fewer trees lined the paths now, and the streetlamps were newer, and sleeker, casting a different light than she remembered. Even the benches were not the same, the weathered wood was replaced by cold, metallic structures.

"Can I just walk around the park?" Luna's voice was soft, but there was a tinge of nostalgia. She wanted to reconnect with the place one last time.

Rafi barely looked up. "I didn't bring you here for a picnic."

"But I want to," Luna pleaded, her voice taking on a childish tone, eyes wide with a hundred cute expressions. "Please."

Rafi sighed, rolling his eyes as he pocketed his phone. "Fine. But no mischief, you hear me? I still have the remote." He patted his pocket menacingly, reminding her of the bomb she carried.

They began walking, the pavement beside the river crunching beneath their feet. The water sparkled in the sunlight, but Luna's mind was far from peaceful. "If you press that, you'll die with me," she said flatly.

Rafi shrugged, not breaking his stride. "Doesn't matter. I know I'm dead either way."

Luna stopped walking and turned to him. "What do you mean?"

"Even if this plan succeeds, I won't be around to enjoy the aftermath. Tonight, after all this, I'll kill myself."

Luna's breath hitched. "But why? Why are you doing this if you're just going to end it all?"

Rafi's face hardened. "Because I can't live without my brother."

Luna blinked back her tears. "Then why do all of this? Why drag me into it?"

"This... this is about waking up our society," Rafi muttered, his voice devoid of the passion Luna expected. He didn't elaborate. His tone made it clear the conversation was over.

They walked in silence, the weight of their shared fate pressing down on them as heavily as the summer heat.

# XXVI
## Chapter 26

**Leo rotated the knob with deliberate precision,**
his eyes fixed on the descending numbers displayed beside it. The cockpit lights cast a dim glow over the instruments, highlighting the beads of sweat forming on his forehead. With a slight push, he engaged the decompression system, accelerating the slow bleed of air from the cabin. The oxygen levels were dropping—faster now.

Leo's fingers danced across the control panel, flicking switches with an eerie calm. Outside, the endless expanse of the sky stretched in every direction, the horizon a fading line between earth and space. The plane had disappeared from civilian radars.

At any moment, the sensors inside the cabin would detect the rapid pressure drop, and oxygen masks would fall from the ceiling. Panic would spread like wildfire. The passengers, without thinking, would latch onto the masks—unaware that poison awaited them in the very air they were supposed to breathe.

Bill sat in silence beside Leo, his body rigid with tension. The once familiar hum of the plane's engines now felt ominous, like the ticking of a clock counting down to their doom. A single gun rested on the table between them, a silent threat. One false move and Leo could end him with a single shot. Bill knew he had to stay alive if there was any chance of saving the passengers. And more than that—he had to save Luna.

He clenched his fists, his mind racing. Then, a flicker of memory hit him. One of the hijackers—one of Leo's men—had mentioned something about a gun in his own bag. Bill shifted in his seat, careful not to alert Leo to his movements.

With painstaking slowness, he slid his chair back slightly and reached for his bag. He kept his gaze forward, his face as neutral as he could manage while his hand rummaged through the fabric of his travel bag.

His fingers brushed against something cold. Metallic. Heavy. Bill's heart skipped a beat as he felt the unmistakable weight of a firearm. Slowly, he wrapped his fingers around it and pulled it out, hoping the noise of the cockpit and the soft hum of electronics masked the sound of the zipper.

Bill's pulse quickened as he brought the gun into view. It was sleek and new, the metal reflecting the dim light of the cockpit. He could almost smell the factory oil on it. Bill had handled weapons before, but this one was different—it was pristine, untouched as if it had never been used. He hesitated for a moment, feeling the unbroken trigger under his finger.

Swallowing hard, Bill raised the pistol, aiming it directly at Leo. His hand trembled slightly, the weight of the decision pressing down on him. Leo's head snapped toward him, his eyes widening in surprise. He pushed himself back into his seat, throwing his hands up in exaggerated surrender.

"Oh my God!" Leo exclaimed, his voice laced with mock panic. "What are you going to do, Bill? Shoot me?" His lips curled into a smirk, amusement dancing in his eyes.

Bill's brow furrowed, but he didn't lower the gun. He pulled the hammer back, the sound loud in the confined space of the cockpit. His finger tightened on the trigger, but just as he was about to fire, Leo burst into laughter—loud, uncontrollable laughter that echoed off the walls.

Bill hesitated, confused. "What's so funny?" he demanded, his grip tightening.

Leo wiped a tear from the corner of his eye, still chuckling. "You really think you've got me, don't you?" He leaned forward, his laughter fading into a smug grin. "Bill, those bullets in your gun? They're rubber. With red ink tips." Leo's eyes sparkled with malicious glee. "A little surprise for you."

Bill's heart sank. He quickly ejected the magazine, and sure enough, the bullets were fake—rubber tips painted red to mimic real ammunition. He cursed under his breath, throwing the useless weapon onto the table. His head thudded back against his seat as frustration clawed at him. Leo's laughter continued a cruel reminder of how powerless Bill felt.

But then Bill's eyes flicked toward the cockpit radar. Something had caught his attention. His breath hitched as he leaned forward, peering through the window. There, in the distance, were four sleek F-16 fighter jets, flanking the plane on either side like silent predators. They were fully armed, their presence unmistakable. Bill knew why they were there.

***"This is Wing Commander Fronx,"*** a low, commanding voice suddenly crackled over the cockpit's communication system. The deep tone was steady, yet the underlying threat was clear.

***"I know you can hear me. We are here to take down the plane. We are aware of First Officer Leo's involvement. Surrender immediately and follow us safely to JFK Airport without harming any passengers. You have no other options. Consider this your first warning."***

Bill's stomach twisted into knots. This was worse than his worst fears. He knew military protocol—knew it far too well. As an air traffic controller, he had been involved in many situations where planes lost communication or veered off course. But he had never, in his entire career, been part of a scenario where the military had to consider shooting down a commercial flight. And yet here they were, following standard procedure.

He also knew something else: there would be three warnings before the jets opened fire. The intervals between the warnings weren't set in stone. They depended entirely on the judgment of the fighter pilots.

Bill stole a glance at Leo, whose eyes were glued to the fighter jets outside. For the first time, Leo looked genuinely rattled, the smugness wiped clean from his face. Bill could see the faintest twitch of fear in the corner of his eyes.

Good, Bill thought. Maybe this situation could still be turned around. The countdown had started, but there was still time—barely.

Leo clenched his jaw, clearly considering his next move. He didn't seem as confident now, and that gave Bill a glimmer of hope.

The military's threat was real, and they didn't bluff. If the situation didn't change soon, those jets would take down the plane without hesitation, and everyone onboard—every innocent passenger—would be caught in the fire. Bill's mind raced. He had to act quickly, but he couldn't afford to be reckless. One wrong move, and not only would Leo kill him, but the jets might intervene sooner than expected.

The oxygen levels were still dropping. The cabin was moments away from decompression. Panic would spread once the masks dropped, and after that, chaos would follow. Bill had to think of something—anything—that could stall Leo or make the situation more manageable.

He looked back at the radar and then at the distant jets, and a small, desperate idea began to form.

# XXVII
## Chapter 27

**Leo pressed the doorbell with his elbow,**
his mouth full of mail, balancing a package awkwardly in his other hand. He fumbled for the doorknob with his free hand, nudging the door open with his shoulder.

As he stepped inside, he kicked off his shoes and wiped his foot absently on the mat. The small, dimly lit apartment greeted him with silence. He walked through the narrow hallway into the cramped living room, the weight of the day heavy on his shoulders.

"Rafi, where are you? I brought your favorite—fried chicken!" Leo called out, his voice echoing slightly in the stillness. He placed the greasy takeout bag on the coffee table and made his way to the fridge.

Grabbing two beers from the door, he popped them open with his teeth, letting the caps clatter to the floor. He slumped into the creaky wooden chair by the table, taking a long sip from his bottle before setting it down with a dull thud.

Pulling out the boxes of chicken, Leo's mouth watered as the familiar scent filled the room. He dipped a wing into the gravy and took a large bite, the rich sauce dripping down his chin. "Sam, dinner's waiting!" he called out again, though there was no Sam.

It was a force of habit from another life, a lifelong gone. As he wiped the corner of his mouth with the back of his hand, his eyes fell on the newspapers stacked on the table.

Odd, he thought. They never got the paper.

Curiosity tugged at him. He reached over, the chicken momentarily forgotten, and picked up the topmost paper. It wasn't in English—some local press, maybe? He glanced at the date. Old. Too old. He rifled through the stack, flipping page after page.

They were from different countries, and different languages, all with various dates. Some were years old. Others were more recent. As he flipped through, a pattern began to emerge. Certain words were underlined, and entire sections were highlighted or circled in red ink. His heart started to race.

He leaned in, staring at the headlines and photos that had been marked. The stories were about war, suffering, and destruction. Every piece told a grim tale of massacres, bombings, and poisoned water supplies.

As his eyes scanned the pages, a cold chill ran down his spine. These were not random. The articles spoke of his homeland, his village, the war that had ravaged everything he'd once known. The destruction of his family. His childhood home.

Suddenly, the realization hit him like a blow to the chest. He knew these stories. They were his stories.

Leo's hands trembled as he dropped the paper, the images flashing before his eyes like ghosts from his past. His heart pounded in his chest. And then it struck him—Rafi. He hadn't responded to his calls. Not once.

"Rafi?" Leo called out, his voice strained. He looked toward the hallway leading to Rafi's bedroom. The door was closed, but a faint light seeped through the cracks.

Rafi never closed his door.

A deep sense of dread settled in Leo's stomach as he stood up, his legs shaky beneath him. "Rafi, you in there?" he asked, though he already knew something was wrong. He knocked once, twice. No answer.

Slowly, he pushed the door open.

At first glance, everything looked normal—until his eyes caught the dark red stains on the floor. Blood. It was pooled by the edge of the bed, trailing across the room like a gruesome breadcrumb path. Leo's breath hitched as he followed the trail with his eyes. His gaze landed on a knife, one that looked eerily familiar. The kitchen knife, he realized. Their kitchen knife.

Besides the knife, Rafi lay slumped in the chair, his arm hanging limply by his side, blood dripping from his wrist in steady, sickening drops. His skin was pale, his face a ghostly shade of white.

"No!" Leo screamed, rushing to his brother's side. He grabbed Rafi's limp wrist, frantically searching for a pulse. For a moment, he couldn't feel anything. His chest tightened with panic, but then—faint. There it was. The faintest beat of life still coursed through Rafi's veins.

"Rafi! What the hell did you do to yourself?" Leo cried, tears blurring his vision as he cradled his brother's body. "How do you think I'm supposed to live without you?"

Rafi's eyes fluttered weakly, barely open. His lips moved, but no sound came out at first. Then, in a raspy, broken whisper, he said, "I... I can't live here... not when our family is dying back home..."

Tears streamed down Leo's face as he held his brother, shaking his head in disbelief. "You're all I have left, Rafi. You're all I have!"

The ambulance arrived soon after, the wail of the sirens piercing through the night air. Medics rushed into the apartment, swiftly placing Rafi on a stretcher and whisking him away. Leo followed in a daze, his shirt soaked with Rafi's blood, his hands trembling uncontrollably. He barely noticed the people around him, the medics asking him questions, the nurses guiding him to the waiting room.

Hours passed, and Leo found himself sitting alone on a cold plastic bench outside the operating room. His thoughts were a chaotic mess. He felt like he was drowning in guilt, in fear, in hopelessness. His eyes were red from crying, and his head heavy with exhaustion.

Absentmindedly, Leo reached into his pocket and pulled out the mail he had grabbed earlier. Among the bills and junk mail, there was a letter with a foreign postmark. His hands shook as he opened it. The handwriting was rough and hurried. It was from his cousin, Kazar, back in their village.

*"Dear Leo,*

*I don't know how to say this, but I can't forget what happened. We were hit hard a few weeks ago. They poisoned the water supply and spread something in the air during the night. It knocked me out for good. The lucky ones ran. Your uncle and I made it to the shelters, but we lost everyone else. Your mother's body was found last week, but your sister... she's still missing. I don't know if she's alive. We've lost everything—our home, our family. I don't know how much longer I can hold on. I hope you're safe, brother.*

*Kazar."*

The letter slipped from Leo's hands, fluttering to the floor. He felt like the air had been sucked from his lungs. His mother was dead. His sister missing, likely gone. His village was destroyed. And here was Rafi, barely clinging to life in a hospital bed because he couldn't bear the weight of it all. Leo let out a heart-wrenching sob, burying his face in his hands.

What was left for him now? His family was gone. His home was destroyed. The thought of ending it all crossed his mind more than once. The idea of simply letting go, of slipping into nothingness, seemed so easy, so comforting.

But then, a flicker of something inside him—something raw and angry—kept him from going further down that dark path. His brother needed him. His family's suffering wouldn't end if he gave up. If anything, he had to fight harder now, for them, for Rafi.

Tears streamed down his face as he clenched his fists.

# XXVIII
## Chapter 28

Aury tied the last strap of the oxygen mask,
her hands trembling slightly as the gravity of the situation weighed heavily on her mind. She had worked with the volunteers to get everything in place, but now, as she walked back toward the front gallery with a handful of leftover zip locks, the tension in the air was palpable.

The passengers, once anxious and fearful, had grown increasingly suspicious. It was clear to everyone on board that something was terribly wrong, and the fact that the crew had been moving with such urgency only fueled their panic.

As Aury stepped into the gallery, she felt the cold, accusing stares of the passengers. It was as if every eye was silently accusing her, blaming her for the crisis unfolding around them. Some of them looked ready to confront her, but fear or confusion kept them glued to their seats. Nobody had the strength to ask questions; they were too afraid of the answers.

Rising on her toes, Aury scanned the crowd. She spotted John and the man with the scarred face standing at the center of a small group of volunteers. The rest of the passengers were scattered across the aisles, some huddled in whispered conversations, others watching silently.

"Everyone, please return to your seats," Aury announced, her voice steady despite the knot in her throat. She felt the weight of responsibility hanging over her, and it was suffocating. She glanced down the aisle to where Carie was serving juice to passengers near the tail of the plane, doing her best to maintain a sense of calm in an atmosphere that felt like it could explode into chaos at any second.

Turning back, Aury noticed John and the scarred man working with the oxygen cylinders and masks, tools spread out across the floor. They were tinkering with something, their movements precise but urgent.

"We did it!" John exclaimed, a note of triumph in his voice. He and the scarred man exchanged a glance, their relief momentarily cutting through the tension.

"We've managed to rig three masks to each cylinder," John continued. "That gives us enough for thirty-six people—just enough for every child and elderly passenger."

The scarred man added with a proud grin, "The credit goes to him and his mechanical knowledge."

Aury couldn't help but smile, despite the gnawing worry in her chest. "Thank you," she said, sincerity in her voice. "You might've just saved their lives."

The man puffed up with pride. "My pleasure. Just doing my part."

Jessica, another flight attendant, was busy rearranging seats in the aisle to group the children and elderly together. Despite the grim situation, there was a flicker of hope. They had a plan; however fragile it was.

But then John's voice dropped to a whisper. "We still have a problem."

Aury and the scarred man both looked at him, confusion flashing across their faces. "What do you mean?" the man asked, reaching for a water bottle from a nearby pile. Just as he was about to take a drink, Aury swiftly snatched the bottle from his hand.

"Are you crazy? These could be poisoned!" she hissed, capping the bottle tightly and tossing it back onto the pile.

John continued, "We may have prepared the cylinders, but we don't actually know what's in them. What if they're filled with poison instead of oxygen?"

Aury's heart sank. Of course. It was a terrifying possibility, one that hadn't occurred to her in the rush to get everything ready. She stared at the tanks, suddenly unsure if they were life-saving tools or ticking time bombs.

"I'll test them," the scarred man volunteered, his voice calm but determined.

"How?" Aury asked, frowning. "We can't just—"

"Simple," the man cut her off. "I'll take a breath from each cylinder. If I survive, we'll know it's safe."

"No!" Aury and John both protested at once. "We can't risk a passenger's life like that!" John added.

"I'm the best one for the job," the scarred man insisted. "If anything happens to me, it won't matter. I've got nothing to lose. You need to stay alive to help the others."

His words hung in the air like a death sentence. The resolve in his eyes was unshakeable, and after a long, tense silence, Aury and John reluctantly agreed.

"Be careful," Aury whispered, her stomach churning with dread.

The scarred man didn't flinch. He pulled a mask from the first cylinder, securing it tightly over his face. John stood beside the tank, his hand trembling slightly as he turned the knob. The sound of hissing gas filled the cabin, and everyone held their breath. The man inhaled deeply through the mask, his eyes closed, his face set in grim determination.

Seconds passed like hours.

Finally, he pulled the mask away and exhaled slowly, opening his eyes. He looked around, blinking. "I'm still here," he said with a half-smile.

A collective sigh of relief swept through the gallery.

They repeated the process with each cylinder, and each time, the scarred man emerged unscathed. By the time they finished, Aury's knees felt weak with relief. None of the cylinders contained poison.

For now, they were safe.

"I think the cabin's decompressing," the man remarked after the last test. "I can feel it now, the air getting thinner."

Aury nodded. "Breathe normally and get some rest. You've done more than enough." John helped the man back to his seat, guiding him gently as the passengers watched.

Suddenly, Aury noticed a change in the atmosphere. The anxious murmurs had been replaced by excited whispers. Passengers were pointing out of the windows, their faces lit with a strange mixture of awe and fear.

Curious, Aury walked toward one of the windows in the business class section and peered outside. Her heart sank.

Fighter jets. Four of them, sleek and menacing, flanked the plane on all sides.

The sight made her blood run cold. The passengers, unaware of the full implications, seemed almost relieved by the presence of the military aircraft. To them, it looked like an escort. But Aury knew better. She had seen this before. This was no escort—it was a death sentence waiting to be carried out if Bill, their captain, didn't respond.

If the plane continued on its current path, there was no question of what would happen next. The jets were there to ensure the safety of those on the ground, not the people on board. The military would give a warning, maybe two, and then, if nothing changed, they would shoot the plane out of the sky.

This was standard procedure for a hijacked aircraft, and Aury knew that if Bill didn't make contact soon, they would all be dead within minutes.

# XXIX

## Chapter 29

**The cockpit fell into an eerie silence,** the hum of the engines barely audible over the weight of the conversation. Leo sat rigid in his seat, eyes locked on the fighter jets that flanked the aircraft. The military jets passed by, cutting through the sky with lethal grace, their presence a constant reminder of the stakes. Bill shifted uncomfortably, watching Leo's expression—a storm of conflicting emotions brewing beneath the surface. He had to find a way to break through, to get through to the friend he once knew.

"I never expected this from you, Leo," Bill said, his voice trembling slightly as he fought to contain his own fear and confusion. Leo continued to gaze outside, his attention fixed on the jets. The weight of Bill's words seemed to hang in the air, unacknowledged.

"Leo," Bill pressed, his voice growing more urgent, "Did you hear me? What in the world is making you do all this? You were never like this. What changed?"

Still no response. Leo's eyes remained glued to the window, watching the military jet glide past as if it were some distant specter, unreal.

"Leo," Bill tried again, his tone softening. "Don't you want to bring your sister and mom to the US? Didn't you want to provide them with a better life? Answer me, Leo. Please... answer me."

A shadow passed over Leo's face, and he finally whispered something under his breath. At first, it was too faint to hear, a broken sound that seemed more like a memory than words.

"They killed them."

Bill's heart skipped a beat. "What?"

"They killed my family!" Leo screamed suddenly, his voice cracking with raw pain. His body shuddered with the force of his emotions, and Bill saw the cracks in his hardened exterior. "The agony they went through... no one knows. No one cared."

Bill blinked, stunned. "What do you mean, Leo? What happened to them?"

Leo's hands tightened around the controls, his knuckles white. His face twisted into a mask of anguish and rage. "Yes, nobody even knows how they suffered. How they killed the innocents! The media? The media never talked about them. All they cared about was how the rich celebrated their New Year, what some celebrity wore to a party!" He spat the words out, his voice thick with bitterness.

Bill felt a chill run down his spine. He had never seen Leo like this. His once calm, collected friend was unraveling before his eyes.

"But if a single American gets tortured or killed," Leo continued, "the whole world is there to show sympathy. The world will bend over backward to mourn them. But my family? My people? They're just... forgotten."

Bill stared at him, the pieces slowly falling into place. "Wait," Bill interrupted gently, trying to steer the conversation back to the heart of the matter. "What exactly happened to your family?"

Leo's breath caught, his eyes welling with tears, but his voice hardened. "They destroyed my country, Bill. They bombed our homes. They poisoned our water and our air. They killed us slowly, day by day. My village, my family, everything I had—it's gone. And no one cared. Not a single person cared."

Bill's chest tightened. He could feel Leo's pain radiating off him, like a storm ready to break. He wanted to reach out, to help somehow, but how do you heal someone whose entire world has been torn apart?

"They bombed us while we slept," Leo continued, his voice quieter now, trembling. "They mixed chemicals into our water. Poisoned our land. My mother, my sister—they never stood a chance."

For a moment, neither of them spoke. The only sound was the quiet beeping of the cockpit instruments and the ever-present hum of the engines. The silence between them was heavy, an abyss filled with grief and anger.

"This is Wing Commander Fronx," came the deep, authoritative voice of the pilot from one of the fighter jets. "I know you can hear me. We request you surrender and follow us safely to JFK without harming a single passenger. Take this as your final warning."

The cockpit echoed with the command, but neither Bill nor Leo moved. The tension hung thick in the air, pressing down on both of them.

"Leo..." Bill started again, choosing his words carefully. "Do you really think what you're doing is right? Do you think killing these people—these innocents—is going to bring your family back?"

Leo's eyes burned with a fierce, quiet rage. "Do I think it's right? No, Bill, I don't. But I don't think what they did to us was right, either. And if I have to make the world see—if I have to make them feel the pain my family felt—then that's what I'll do."

Bill felt his heart sink. He could hear the desperation in Leo's voice, the hopelessness that had driven him to this point. But he knew that if Leo went through with this, if he crashed the plane, nothing would be solved. It would only create more pain and more suffering.

"Leo," Bill said, his voice soft, pleading. "Killing these passengers—it's not the solution. It won't solve anything. But if we stay alive, maybe we can find another way. There has to be a way out of this that doesn't involve more innocent lives being lost."

Leo looked at Bill, his face twisted in anguish. "Solution? Do you think there's a solution? From who? From those who don't even care if we live or die? They won't care about what happens here today, Bill. It's too late for that. And I know it would be hard for Luna to live without you. I know." His voice softened for a moment, and Bill saw a flicker of the old Leo, the man he once trusted with his life. "But I had no other option."

"You do have another option, Leo. I promise you," Bill said, his voice steady, holding onto the last thread of hope. "If you let this go, I'll help you. I'll do whatever I can to make things right. But you have to stop this. You have to trust me."

"No!" Leo's face hardened again, and his hand moved to the control panel. He turned the knob slightly further, and the numbers on the altimeter continued to drop. The plane was descending faster now, and Bill's heart raced with panic.

"I want them to feel it," Leo muttered, his eyes fixed on the control panel. "I want them to know how my family suffered. An impact big enough to make them pay attention. To make them understand."

Bill's mind raced, desperately searching for something, anything that could stop Leo. He couldn't let this happen—not to the passengers, not to Luna, and not to Leo.

# XXX

## Chapter 30

The cockpit felt like a tomb.

No sound but the hum of the engines and the distant, muted warnings from the fighter jets. Bill sat there, paralyzed, his mind racing in a desperate search for anything that could stop what was coming. He had tried everything—reason, empathy, memories—but Leo was lost in his grief and rage, unreachable.

The time was slipping away, and with each second, they drew closer to New York. The city, vibrant and alive, lay beneath them, unaware of the horror hurtling toward it from the sky.

They had already received two warnings from the military jets. The third, Bill knew, would be their last. If Leo didn't stop, they wouldn't have to worry about crashing the plane—because the jets would take it down first.

Bill's stomach churned at the thought of it: the passengers, the families, all of them dying either way. Whether it was Leo or the fighter jets didn't matter. He was flying a coffin full of innocent people, and he couldn't save them.

Bill's hand trembled as he reached into his pocket and pulled out his wallet. Inside was a worn photograph, the edges frayed from years of being handled. It was his family—Lucia holding little Luna, both smiling in the sunlight. He traced his finger over the picture, his heart breaking. Tears welled up in his eyes as he whispered, "I'm so sorry, dear. I failed you. I couldn't keep my promise."

His breath hitched as he held the photograph, his mind filled with memories of his wife and daughter, the life he had promised to protect. Now, it felt as though he had let them down in the most devastating way.

"I want to talk to Luna," Bill said, his voice cracking under the weight of emotion.

Leo turned to him, momentarily snapping out of his trance. For a moment, he just stared, then nodded slowly. "Okay," he whispered. There was a brief pause as Leo typed something into his phone, and Bill's heart raced. "I'll let you speak to her. Your last wish will be granted."

Seconds later, Bill's phone buzzed. A video call from Luna's mobile. His hands fumbled as he quickly answered the call. The moment her face appeared on the screen; his heart clenched. She was sitting on a park bench, her eyes red from crying, trying to be brave for him.

"Sweetheart," Bill said, his voice shaking. "Are you okay? Are you safe?"

"I'm fine, Daddy. I'm okay," Luna said, wiping away a tear with her sleeve. She was wearing a black coat, and huddled under a tree. "How are you, Daddy? When are you coming home?"

Bill swallowed the lump in his throat. "Luna, honey, listen to me. Daddy might not come home after this flight." His voice broke, but he forced himself to stay calm for her sake. "I don't have another option, sweetheart. Things... things are complicated right now."

"Daddy, no!" Luna cried, shaking her head, the tears coming faster. "Don't say that! Please come back. I need you."

Bill's heart shattered. He could barely hold it together. "I love you so much, Luna," he said, his voice thick with emotion. "I need you to be strong, okay? Uncle Rafi will take care of you. He'll make sure you get to your aunt's house safely."

As he spoke, something strange caught his eye on the screen. Behind Luna, through her tears and the chaos, there was a familiar sight. The river, the skyline of the buildings across it, the park where she sat—it all clicked into place. Bill felt a jolt of recognition.

The East River.

Bill's mind raced, piecing it together in a flash. The place she was sitting—it was East River State Park. Luna's favorite park, the place where she played as a child, where they had spent so many happy afternoons. The place where he had met Lucia. He had memories tied to every corner of that park. How could he not have realized it sooner?

The image of the park, serene and peaceful, clashed violently with the terror of the cockpit. Bill stared at the screen, his mind flooded with memories, and his heart broke even further.

"I'm so sorry, sweetheart," Bill whispered, barely holding back the sobs. "I'm sorry I made this the worst birthday of your life."

Before Luna could say anything, Bill ended the call. He couldn't bear to hear her cry any longer, knowing there was nothing he could do to make things better. He closed his eyes, trying to suppress the wave of grief that threatened to consume him.

But then, a sudden realization dawned on him. **Luna was at the park!** The same park that was close enough to be in danger if anything went wrong with the plane. A surge of adrenaline shot through him. He had to do something.

Bill flipped open the cover of his iPad, hands shaking. He reached for his headset, which sat beside him, careful not to alert Leo. His fingers fumbled with the mic for a second before he finally activated it.

"Can you hear me?" Bill whispered urgently; his voice low but firm. "I need help. Please."

He paused, his breath coming in short, panicked bursts. He looked over at Leo, who was engrossed in calculating the distance to Times Square. There was no time.

**"Luna is in East River State Park. I repeat—she's in East River State Park,"** Bill continued, his voice shaking with desperation. "Please save her. It's the Marsha P. Johnson State Park. Please, someone—**save her.**"

Bill's eyes darted back to the window, where the fighter jets still flanked them on either side. One was directly above the plane, positioned to strike at any moment. The others hovered close behind, their deadly purpose clear on the radar in front of him. They were perfectly aligned to take down the aircraft if they received the order.

His mind raced. There was nothing else he could do but wait. Would anyone hear him? Would they be able to save Luna in time? He had sent out the only lifeline he had left, and now it was up to fate.

# XXXI

## Chapter 31

**The situation in the command center was tense,** an electric charge of anticipation hanging in the air. Hud kept his headset glued to his ear, scribbling down notes in a hurried flurry as everyone watched with bated breath. Hoffs' nervous tapping stopped; his hand frozen in place on the globe on Sofia's desk. Even Sofia, typically composed, had a look of dread that deepened with each passing second.

"We will wait for another few minutes before we give the last warning," Hud had said, but those minutes stretched thin, the weight of the decisions before them felt like a crushing force.

Hoffs finally broke the silence. "Any word from Bill?" His voice was terse, eyes darting between the people in the room.

"Nothing," Sofia replied, pacing by the window. "We've already had two calls from the White House, and they're demanding answers. They want to know why we haven't taken action yet. I don't know what to tell them." Her frustration was palpable. "They're expecting results."

Suddenly, Hud jerked forward, adjusting his headset, his body stiffening as if electrified by the voice in his ear. "Wait," he whispered sharply, motioning for silence.

His face, bathed in concentration, was unreadable, but his posture was enough to silence everyone in the room. The tension grew unbearable as he started jotting down dots and lines—morse code. Each stroke of the pen felt like it carried the weight of a life.

Everyone's eyes were glued to Hud, especially Hoffs, who had inched closer to see the message unfold. Dot by dot, line by line. The letters slowly formed into words, the urgency growing with each symbol revealed. Hoffs' breath caught in his throat as the realization hit him like a freight train.

"What the hell..." Hoffs muttered under his breath, adrenaline spiking as he ran his hand through his hair. Without wasting another second, he bolted for the door, pulling out his phone and barking orders into it as he sprinted down the stairs. The situation had just escalated far beyond what any of them had expected.

Sofia stood frozen, then rushed to Hud's side, her eyes scanning the message on the paper. As the final word clicked into place, her complexion turned pale. It was Luna. Bill had revealed her location—the East River State Park. The Marsha P. Johnson State Park. And she wasn't just in the park; she was in danger. There was a kidnapper involved.

Hud exchanged a silent, grave look with Sofia. Time was no longer on their side.

---

Meanwhile, Hoffs was already in his car, the engine roaring as he floored the gas pedal. Sweat poured down his face, the seatbelt strap feeling tight across his chest as the sirens wailed from his vehicle. Every second felt like an eternity, each one potentially the difference between life and death for Luna—and for everyone else on the plane.

How had Bill known she was there? He didn't have time to puzzle it out. He just knew Bill was right, and that he had to get to the park before it was too late. His mind was racing as fast as the engine, weaving through the narrow streets, barely avoiding collisions with slower-moving vehicles. He had one goal now: Get to Luna before the kidnapper could move her again.

But then, the inevitable happened—traffic. The streets of New York were clogged, packed with endless lines of honking, frustrated cars. Hoffs gritted his teeth, the red lights taunting him as the seconds ticked away. He could almost hear the clock ticking down in his head.

He pressed his foot hard against the gas pedal, the engine roaring as the light turned yellow. Desperation clouded his judgment. He couldn't wait.

Suddenly, as he shot into the intersection, a bus smashed into the side of his car, the force of the impact spinning his vehicle violently across the street. Everything blurred. Glass shattered; metal crunched. The air was filled with the screeching of tires and the sickening sound of the crash.

The world around him stopped. Dazed, Hoffs blinked, blood trickling from a cut on his forehead. His car was wrecked and crumpled into the side of the intersection. Bystanders rushed toward the scene, and the sound of sirens grew louder as emergency responders neared.

"Are you okay?" someone shouted, pulling at his door.

But Hoffs didn't have time for concern. He knew the stakes. His hand reached up to his head, touching the blood, but his mind was clear. He needed to keep moving.

Ignoring the pain, he unbuckled his seatbelt and staggered out of the car. Around him, the wreckage was chaotic—another vehicle was flipped, and a motorcyclist lay unconscious on the pavement. But Hoffs couldn't focus on them. Luna. He had to save Luna.

Then he saw it. A motorcycle, lying on its side, just outside the debris. Without hesitating, he sprinted over, dragging the bike upright and straddling it. His hands shook as he hit the ignition, the engine roaring to life beneath him.

"I'm sorry, dude," Hoffs muttered as he revved the engine, "but I'm borrowing your bike."

With a quick flick of the throttle, the motorcycle shot forward, weaving between the now-motionless cars. The sirens behind him faded into the distance as he raced toward the East River State Park, his body leaning with every tight corner. People turned to watch as the loud rumble of the bike echoed through the streets, but Hoffs didn't care about the attention. He was a man on a mission.

The roads blurred around him as his speed increased, adrenaline pumping through his veins. The city streets seemed like a blur of noise and light, but his focus was razor-sharp. His mind raced with possibilities, but there was no time for doubt. He pushed through the traffic, bouncing over curbs, and dodging pedestrians. He had to reach Luna in time.

Finally, he saw the entrance to the park. Skidding to a stop, Hoffs jumped off the bike, sprinting past the guards who barely had time to react. He ignored their shouts, his feet pounding on the pavement as he raced into the park.

He scanned the park frantically as he sprinted past the benches and trees, searching for any sign of Luna. The tranquil beauty of the riverside clashed violently with the chaos in his mind. People screamed as he tore past them, weaving through the families and couples lounging in the grass.

Then, as he crested a small hill near the riverbank, he froze. He had reached the water's edge, his eyes scanning the area. Where was Luna?

His heart pounded in his chest as he searched desperately. She had to be here.

But something felt off.

# XXXII
## Chapter 32

**Luna's heart raced as she sat frozen on the bench,**
staring at the screen that had just gone dark after the heartbreaking conversation with her father. Tears streamed down her face as she tried to comprehend everything Bill had said. Next to her, Rafi sat in silence, offering a tissue with a soft yet distant gesture. Despite his rugged appearance—unkempt beard, disheveled uniform, and the menacing aura of a villain—there was something unnervingly human about him. But Luna knew better than to be fooled by his momentary kindness.

"I know it's hard," Rafi said, his voice soft but firm. "I'm sorry, but I think this was written in your destiny." Luna's tear-streaked face turned toward him, feeling the weight of those words like a heavy blanket of sorrow.

As Rafi's phone buzzed, Luna's attention drifted to the blinking red light on the remote clipped to his belt. Her hands, though bound, flexed subtly at the sight. She hadn't noticed it before, but now, the blinking light was all she could focus on. The remote—the key to whatever was happening on that plane. The only chance she had was to stop it.

Her mind raced. Could she grab it? She glanced at Rafi, still distracted by the call. She shifted slightly closer, moving slowly, inch by inch, trying not to attract his attention. Her breath hitched as her fingers brushed the fabric of his jacket, so close to the remote that her pulse quickened with anticipation.

But Rafi wasn't as distracted as she had hoped. He turned sharply, his eyes narrowing, catching her just in time. "Why do people always try to act smart when you give them a little kindness?" he said, his voice hardening as he pulled the gun from his waist in one swift motion.

Luna recoiled, her heart hammering in her chest. The barrel of the gun gleamed under the darkening sky as Rafi aimed it directly at her. Her breath came in shallow gasps, tears welling in her eyes. This was it. She braced herself, closing her eyes, waiting for the inevitable.

Then, like a flash of lightning, the moment shattered.

A sudden gust of wind swept through, and in an instant, the world around her exploded into chaos. The gun was no longer pointed at her; in fact, Rafi was no longer standing at all. A massive figure had collided with him, sending both men crashing to the ground.

Luna blinked in shock, her breath catching in her throat. The massive man was on top of Rafi, pinning him down with ease. His hands, thick and calloused, wrapped around Rafi's throat with a grip so firm that Rafi struggled helplessly beneath him. It was like watching a lion subdue its prey.

The giant man, Officer Hoffs, grunted as he easily disarmed Rafi, tossing the gun aside with a flick of his wrist. His free hand reached for the remote on Rafi's belt and threw it toward Luna. She caught it, adrenaline surging through her veins. Without wasting a moment, she scrambled back to a safer distance, clutching the remote tightly in her bound hands. She had it. The one thing that could stop this nightmare from unfolding.

But the struggle wasn't over.

Rafi was far from defeated. With a sudden burst of strength, he kicked Hoffs hard in the ribs, causing him to groan in pain and lean to the side. In that split second, Rafi saw his chance. He stretched out, his fingers barely grazing the gun that lay in the grass. Just as he grabbed it, Hoffs yanked him back by the leg, hurling him onto the bench with a sickening thud.

They both scrambled to their feet, facing each other. Rafi's eyes blazed with fury, and he lunged forward, swinging a punch that connected with Hoffs' already bruised ribs. The officer staggered back, his breath wheezing as he tried to recover.

"Luna, run!" Hoffs gasped, his voice hoarse with pain.

Luna didn't need to be told twice. She ran.

Her feet pounded against the pavement as she tore through the park, panic gripping her like a vice. Her breath came in ragged bursts, and her bound hands made it difficult to keep balance, but she didn't stop. She couldn't stop. Not with Rafi still after her.

Rafi was right behind her, his eyes wild with rage and desperation. The gun gleamed in his hand, and his heavy footsteps thundered against the ground. Luna could hear him getting closer, his breath hot on the back of her neck. This was life or death.

Hoffs, despite the pain radiating through his chest, refused to give up. He pushed himself up, adrenaline pumping through him, and sprinted after them. His larger frame allowed him to cover the ground quickly, but he knew he only had moments before Rafi caught Luna.

Luna could hear Rafi's footsteps getting louder, his presence looming just behind her. So close. Too close.

Then, in one final desperate move, Hoffs leaped. His body flew over the bench, landing just behind Rafi. He stretched out, his fingers grazing the fabric of Rafi's shirt, and with one last burst of energy, he yanked him back, throwing him off balance. Rafi stumbled but managed to twist around, his gun raising as he aimed at Luna.

"No!" Hoffs bellowed, forcing himself forward even though his body screamed in pain. He reached Rafi just as the gun fired.

The shot rang out through the park, echoing off the buildings and sending birds flying into the sky. Time seemed to freeze as Luna stumbled, her eyes wide with shock, unsure if she had been hit.

But the bullet hadn't found its mark.

Hoffs had tackled Rafi just in time, slamming into him with the full force of his body. The gunshot had gone wild, missing Luna by inches. They crashed to the ground, a tangled mess of limbs and violence. The gun slipped from Rafi's hand once more, and this time, Hoffs wasn't letting him get it back.

With a final, bone-crushing punch, Hoffs knocked Rafi unconscious. The man slumped to the ground, motionless.

Breathing heavily, Hoffs stood, his chest heaving as he looked around. It was over. He looked at Luna, who stood trembling a few feet away, clutching the remote like her life depended on it.

She met his eyes, her expression a mix of shock and relief. They had survived.

But as the adrenaline began to wear off, Luna realized something with a sinking feeling. The remote. She had it—but what could she do with it? There was still the plane, still her father, still the poison in the air.

And time was running out.

# XXXIII

## Chapter 33

**The sky was painted in hues of orange and gold as the sun dipped low on the horizon,**
casting long shadows across the park. The trees rustled in the growing wind, their leaves fluttering like whispers of something ominous in the air.

The tension was palpable as Rafi stood several yards away from Officer Hoffs, holding Luna tightly against his chest. His arm was locked around her throat, and the barrel of his gun was pressed firmly against her temple. One wrong move from Hoffs, one misstep, and Luna would be gone.

Hoffs didn't have a gun. His breath was shallow, his heart pounding in his chest as his mind raced for a solution. There wasn't time to think. He locked eyes with Rafi, silently pleading for some sign of weakness, anything that would give him an opening. But Rafi's face was stone cold, and his resolve was chilling. He took a slow step backward, inching away from Hoffs, widening the gap between them.

Hoffs knew he couldn't let him take Luna any further. The distance would give Rafi more control, and more room to maneuver. Hoffs had to act, even if it meant risking everything. Without a second thought, he took a deep breath, pushed off his back foot, and sprinted toward Rafi with everything he had. It was now or never.

Luna's eyes widened in fear, her body shrinking into Rafi's chest as she felt the gun press harder against her temple. She closed her eyes, bracing herself for what she thought was the inevitable.

Then, the gunshot rang out.

The sharp crack echoed through the park, reverberating off the trees and startling the birds from their perches. They scattered into the sky with frantic wings, chirping in alarm as they disappeared into the orange glow of the sunset.

Hoffs froze in his tracks. His heart stopped, fear paralyzing him. He stood there, motionless, waiting for the awful reality to sink in. He dreaded the sight of Luna's lifeless body crumpling to the ground.

But it wasn't Luna who fell.

With a heavy thud, Rafi's body collapsed to the ground behind her, blood pooling beneath him. The gun slipped from his hand, landing silently in the grass. Luna stood in shock, her eyes wide and her breath shallow. She hadn't been hit. Her body trembled violently, her mind struggling to process what had just happened.

Hoffs snapped out of his daze and sprinted to her. He grabbed her in a tight embrace, holding her as she collapsed against him, sobbing into his chest. Her whole body shook, but she was alive. She was safe. He stroked her hair gently, whispering, "It's okay, Luna. You're safe now."

But how? How had Rafi been shot? Hoffs glanced around, confusion etched on his face, and then he saw her.

Lara stood several yards away, her hands trembling but steady enough to hold the smoking gun in her grasp. Beside her, Amelia held her by the shoulder, supporting her as she lowered the weapon. Lara's face was pale, her breath shaky, but there was no mistaking what she had done. She had taken the shot.

Lara and Amelia hurried over to Luna, who was still clutching onto Hoffs, her tears soaking his shirt. Lara knelt beside her, offering her a bottle of water. Luna gulped it down, the cool liquid calming her nerves slightly as she fought to steady her breath.

"Everything's going to be fine, Luna," Lara reassured her, her voice soft and soothing. Amelia sat beside her, trying to help pull the heavy jacket off Luna's trembling body.

As the immediate danger passed, questions began to flood everyone's mind. "What do you mean the first officer was involved the whole time?" Amelia asked, her voice thick with disbelief.

Hoffs let out a deep sigh as he pulled a crumpled photograph from his pocket, showing it to both women. "His name is Leo," he said, watching as their eyes widened in shock. "Leo was in on it from the beginning."

"Uncle Leo?" they both exclaimed, looking from the photo to each other. Luna's tears stopped for a moment, replaced by disbelief. "But Daddy never mentioned anything about him!" she cried. "We haven't seen him in years! How could it be him?"

Hoffs shook his head. "I know it's hard to believe, but it's true. Leo orchestrated the entire thing. We'll get to the bottom of why he did it, but for now, we have to focus on what's next."

Before they could dwell on the revelation, the unmistakable sound of sirens filled the air. Police cars and bomb squad vehicles arrived, the flashing lights casting eerie shadows across the park. FBI agents swarmed the area, closing it off with yellow tape and evacuating civilians.

The bomb squad, in their thick green suits, moved toward Luna, surrounding her as they carefully unzipped the dangerous jacket she wore. Each wire was examined meticulously before they slowly, cautiously, pulled the device off her body and secured it in a large containment box.

Luna exhaled deeply as the weight of the bomb was lifted from her shoulders, both physically and emotionally. She sagged onto the bench, her body finally relaxing for the first time in what felt like hours.

On the other side of the park, paramedics tended to Hoffs, cleaning his wounds and wrapping bandages around his shoulders. Hoffs winced as they wiped at the blood on his head, but his mind was elsewhere. He barely noticed the nurse working on him until

Luna approached, taking the cotton from her hand and gently wiping the wound herself.

"Are you okay?" she asked, her voice soft but filled with gratitude.

Hoffs smiled through the pain. "I'll live. Thanks to Lara, not me. She saved us both today." Luna finished sticking the bandage on him and gave a small, grateful nod, looking over at Lara with a mix of awe and respect.

"They're going to crash the plane into Times Square," Lara interrupted, her voice tense as she approached with a phone to her ear. "The authorities are evacuating the area, but there's no telling how long they have."

"We need to go," Hoffs said, rising to his feet, grimacing through the pain. "Now."

Luna and Amelia hurried after him, while Lara quickly pocketed her phone. "Where are we going?" Amelia asked as they neared a car.

"Times Square?" Luna suggested, glancing nervously at Hoffs.

Hoffs shook his head. "No. JFK Airport."

"Do you really think you can drive like that?" Lara asked, eyeing Hoffs' wounded body.

He paused, looking at his bruised hands and aching limbs, before sighing in defeat. Lara smirked, pushed him aside, and slid into the driver's seat. "Let's go, then," she said, revving the engine as the rest of them piled into the car.

The tires screeched as they sped out of the park, dust, and gravel kicking up behind them as they raced through the streets.

# XXXIV
## Chapter 34

**Aury leaned back in her seat,**
finally able to exhale after what felt like hours of tense anticipation. The plane had been rocking violently through turbulence, but the notifications on her phone had pulled her out of the chaos in her mind. She scrolled through a series of messages from Hoffs and Amelia, her hands trembling slightly.

"Luna is safe! The bad guy is killed."

That was the last message from Amelia, accompanied by a photo of them sitting in the backseat of a car. Relief washed over Aury, bringing a fleeting moment of happiness to her otherwise frantic state. She hadn't realized how much tension had been stored in her body until she felt the joy rush through her veins. Luna was safe.

She immediately turned her attention to the cockpit. Bill needed to know. With renewed energy, she rushed to the door and knocked, waiting for a response. But there was nothing. No reply. She knocked again, louder this time, but the door remained locked and silent.

Anxiety began to creep back in. Why weren't they responding? By the time she knocked a third time, John had joined her, his face reflecting the same concern. They exchanged uneasy glances as they tried again to get a response from the cockpit. Nothing.

Her phone buzzed again in her pocket, another message from Amelia lighting up the screen.

"Uncle Leo is the culprit on the plane."

Aury's heart stopped. The words on the screen didn't seem real. Her mind raced as she showed the message to John. His face mirrored the shock she felt. Leo? The man they had trusted for so long, the man they'd never suspected. How could this be?

The plane jerked again, and Aury felt a wave of dizziness wash over her. She lost her balance, her legs giving out beneath her. John caught her just in time, helping her to sit in a nearby seat. Her head spun, and she struggled to catch her breath. Around her, she noticed passengers gasping for air, their faces pale with panic. The cabin was decompressing. The oxygen levels were dropping fast.

They didn't have much time.

"We need to unlock the cockpit door," Aury whispered, her voice shaky. John nodded; his face grim. They both knew the risks, but there was no other option. If they didn't get into the cockpit, it would be too late.

John moved to the keypad outside the cockpit door, his fingers working quickly as he typed in the emergency override code. "How long do we have?" Aury asked, her voice barely audible above the sound of her rapid breathing.

"Thirty seconds," John replied, glancing at the loading bar on the small screen above the keypad. "Maybe a minute."

The chime from the keypad echoed through the silence of the cabin as the timer began. Aury's heart pounded in her chest, each second stretching into eternity.

---

Inside the cockpit, darkness had fallen as the plane descended below the thick clouds. The sun, once brilliant and orange, was now hidden behind a dense layer of gray, casting long shadows over the two men seated in the cockpit.

Bill's breathing had become labored, each breath feeling more difficult than the last. The cabin's decompression was affecting him, too, and the thin air made his head spin. He could see the city sprawled out beneath them now, lights twinkling like stars on the ground. And in the distance, unmistakable, was Times Square—their target.

Across from him, Leo sat with cold determination, his hand hovering near the controls. The green light on the autopilot button labeled AP1 blinked slowly. Without a word, Leo pressed it, disengaging the autopilot. The light went out.

Bill's stomach dropped as the plane lurched, beginning its final descent. Leo gripped the joystick beside him and angled the nose of the aircraft down. They were now below the clouds, and the city's lights grew larger, sharper, more defined. Bill could see the grid of streets, the glowing billboards, the bustling heart of Times Square ahead of them.

There was no time left.

Bill's mind raced. He had thought of everything—every possible way to take control of the situation—but nothing had worked. He glanced at the gun sitting between Leo and him. So close, yet so far.

His thoughts drifted to Lara, Aury, Luna, the passengers—all the lives that depended on him at that moment. The images of their faces flashed before him, and tears welled in his eyes. He couldn't save them. Not like this. Not with Leo in control.

Then a chime rang out from the control panel, a signal that someone was trying to access the cockpit. Leo turned his gaze to the door, his hand hovering over the deny entry button.

This was Bill's chance.

Summoning every ounce of strength he had left, Bill lunged for the joystick beside him, yanking it sharply to the left. The plane veered violently, tipping on its side. The sudden shift in gravity sent everything inside the cockpit flying into the air. For a split second, Bill felt weightless as the gun soared into the air.

Before Leo could react, Bill grabbed the gun mid-air, his hands shaking but steady. He aimed it directly at Leo, his finger tightening on the trigger.

But Leo was fast. His hand darted out, grabbing a pen that had floated free, and he stabbed it into Bill's arm. Bill let out a cry of pain, his finger squeezing the trigger reflexively. The sound of the gunshot was deafening in the small space. Leo's body jerked as the bullet tore through his skull, blood splattering across the cockpit as his body slumped over.

Bill gasped for air, his arm searing with pain, but there was no time to stop. He reached for the autopilot button, slamming his hand down on AP1. The plane stabilized, leveling out just as it hurtled past Times Square. Bill's breath came in short, ragged gasps as he guided the plane back under control, narrowly avoiding disaster.

---

Outside the cockpit, heads turned in confusion as the massive aircraft roared overhead, missing Times Square by a matter of feet. The people below had no idea how close they had come to catastrophe. Sirens wailed, fighter jets zoomed past in formation, but the immediate danger had passed.

Back in the cabin, Aury and John, along with the passengers, felt the plane level out. The oppressive weight of doom lifted, and there was a collective exhale as the realization hit.

They had survived. But it wasn't over yet.

Bill, bloodied and exhausted, took one final glance at Leo's lifeless body before keying in a distress signal. They had made it past Times Square, but the fight wasn't over. The plane still needed to land, and the whole world was watching.

# XXXV
## Chapter 35

John slammed his forehead against the door beside him, a look of sheer frustration etched on his face as the plane continued its erratic roll to the left. Aury, struggling to maintain her balance, clung to her seat with white-knuckled hands. The cabin was in chaos.

The sudden descent and the low oxygen levels made it nearly impossible for anyone to stay calm. Passengers screamed in panic, some fainting from the stress, while others were hunched over their vomit bags, their faces pale with fear.

The terrifying silence was abruptly broken by the sound of gunfire coming from the cockpit. The shriek of a bullet echoing through the confined space only intensified the sense of impending doom.

"Bill!" Aury screamed, her voice filled with terror and desperation. She slammed against the cockpit door with renewed vigor, her fists pounding against the metal as if her strength alone could force it open.

John, his face grim, had managed to pry open a panel beside the door, revealing a small emergency keypad. "Twenty seconds," he said, his voice strained as he typed in the override code. The seconds ticked down with agonizing slowness.

"Fifteen," he continued, his eyes fixed on the display. Aury, heart racing, could barely focus as she heard the door's electronic lock disengage. A sharp click echoed through the cabin, and the door swung open.

Without a second thought, Aury pushed through, her eyes immediately drawn to the scene of devastation within the cockpit. Blood smeared across the floor, painting a grim picture of the violence that had just occurred. "Bill!" she cried out again, her voice breaking.

Bill was slumped in his seat, clutching his left bicep with his right hand, his face contorted in pain. Blood seeped through his fingers and dripped down his arm. The gun that had been used lay discarded on the floor, a grim reminder of the earlier confrontation.

Leo, slumped in his seat, was lifeless, his eyes staring vacantly towards the ceiling. The gaping wound on his forehead was a brutal testament to the fatal shot he had received. Aury's heart ached at the sight, and she instinctively closed Leo's eyes with her hand, turning his face away from Bill.

"John, get the first aid kit quickly!" Aury called out urgently. Her hands were steady as she began to tend to Bill's wounds. She pulled out a bandage and started to wrap his arm, her movements precise but hurried.

Bill, wincing in pain, managed to point to a dial near Leo's seat. "Turn the dial to its maximum," he instructed, his voice strained but determined. Aury nodded and twisted the dial. The cabin's atmosphere began to stabilize as the oxygen levels improved, and the passengers, who had been struggling for breath, started to breathe easier. Jessica, a flight attendant, took charge, guiding the panicked passengers through breathing exercises.

Bill grasped the joystick firmly, maneuvering the aircraft with focused precision. "Full flaps," he ordered. Aury pulled the small white lever to its maximum position, and the landing gear began to extend with a mechanical whir. Green lights on the control panel blinked, indicating that the gear was securely in place. The plane's vibrations were palpable as the landing gear engaged.

"Approaching Minimums," the Ground Proximity Warning System announced, and Aury felt a surge of adrenaline. She had never been so close to the controls of a plane during a landing before.

"Fifty," Bill called out, his voice steady despite his pain. "Forty," he continued, his focus unwavering. "Thirty," the cockpit echoed as the plane's wheels made contact with the runway. The landing gear scraped against the tarmac, and the plane bounced once before Bill expertly adjusted the controls to stabilize the landing.

"Pull them to zero," Bill directed, his voice taut with effort. Aury pulled the thrust levers to their minimum position and then followed up by operating the small levers on top of them to engage the reverse thrusters. The plane shuddered as the engines reversed thrust, slowing the aircraft rapidly.

Bill adjusted several knobs, managing the brakes and guiding the plane to a complete stop on the runway. The cockpit was filled with the sound of clapping from the passengers, their relief and gratitude palpable as they realized they were safely on the ground.

Aury finished bandaging Bill's arm and offered him a reassuring smile. "We made it," she said, her voice trembling with emotion. Bill nodded, his eyes reflecting both exhaustion and relief.

The plane came to a halt, and the emergency services quickly arrived on the scene. Fire trucks, ambulances, and police vehicles surrounded the aircraft as the passengers disembarked, their faces filled with a mix of shock and relief.

As Aury and John stepped out of the plane, the bright lights of JFK Airport illuminated their faces. The ordeal was over, but the memory of the chaos and bravery would linger long after the night had ended.

# XXXVI

## Chapter 36

**The sky darkened as the sun dipped below the horizon,**
casting a deep blue cloak over the scene at JFK Airport. The powerful headlights of the fire trucks cut through the gloom, illuminating the runway and creating a stark contrast against the night sky. The emergency lights flashed rhythmically, painting a surreal picture of chaos and relief.

John, with a determined look, pushed open the door of the plane. A powerful hiss signaled the deployment of the emergency slides. The slides inflated rapidly, and the first passengers, those with visible injuries or needing urgent medical attention, began their descent.

Paramedics and firemen waited at the bottom, their faces illuminated by the bright lights, ready to assist. The second wave of passengers followed, sliding down with a mix of fear and relief, while Jessica, calm and composed, helped pull the straps to deploy the slides from the back of the plane.

The scene was a mix of frantic energy and controlled chaos. The fire trucks began their task, creating arcs of water that shimmered in the lights, forming a rainbow that added a surreal touch to the night. The smell of jet fuel mingled with the acrid scent of smoke, but the immediate danger had passed.

As the last of the passengers slid down and were attended to, Aury turned her attention to Bill, who remained seated, his shirt stained with a mix of his own and Leo's blood. Aury, with John's help, supported Bill as he slowly rose from his seat.

His movements were stiff, his face a mask of exhaustion and pain. He looked around the empty cabin, the oxygen masks dangling uselessly from their compartments, a stark reminder of the chaos that had unfolded. The cabin was a mess—water bottles were strewn in one corner, and everything that wasn't strapped down was thrown to the left side of the aircraft due to the sudden maneuver.

John helped Bill to the door. Bill clutched the handle for support, and together they made their way to the slide. The flashes of cameras from the crowd below lit up the night like a strobe light show. Bill's hand throbbed painfully, but he ignored the paramedics' offers for immediate care, determined to make it through the throng of reporters and onlookers.

As they descended the slide, the scene outside was chaotic yet oddly beautiful. Fire trucks continued to spray the plane with water, creating a shimmering curtain. The rainbow that appeared in the spray was a hopeful symbol amidst the chaos.

When they reached the ground, Bill's movements were labored. Drops of blood trailed behind him as he walked. Reporters and camera crews swarmed around him, shouting questions.

"What connections do you have with the terrorists?" one reporter yelled over the din.

Bill paused, his expression somber. He pulled the mic towards him and said, "He was my best friend." His voice carried a deep, sorrowful weight.

Another reporter asked, "How do you feel about saving every passenger on the plane?"

Bill's gaze fell to the ground. "Yes, I saved everyone, everyone except one. Leo," he said quietly. His voice faltered as he spoke Leo's name, the weight of his loss heavy in his words. He didn't answer any further questions, his focus now solely on moving through the crowd.

Across the way, Luna stood with an FBI agent and Hud, her former colleague. Tears welled up in her eyes as she saw Bill. She ran to him and embraced him tightly, her shoulders shaking with her sobs. Bill hugged her back, his own eyes moist with relief and fatigue.

"This is Hoffs, FBI," the agent introduced himself with a nod.

Hud, recognizing the gravity of the situation, approached with a smile. "You were always the best at Morse," he said, his voice warm and full of admiration. The group shared a moment of mutual respect and camaraderie, their smiles masking the tension and exhaustion of the past hours.

Amelia, having found Aury, threw her arms around her in a tight hug. Tears streamed down her face as she scolded her for the worry she had caused. Despite the seriousness of the situation, the group couldn't help but laugh through their tears at Amelia's emotional outburst. "Thanks for taking care of my daughter," Aury said, her voice trembling with gratitude.

Lara, who had been a rock through the ordeal, finally allowed herself to cry. Her tears mingled with the laughter of the group, a bittersweet release of pent-up emotion.

As the initial wave of relief and gratitude settled, Bill suddenly staggered, his face pale and his breathing labored. Hoffs and Hud rushed to his side, supporting him as he swayed. The paramedics, ever vigilant, quickly moved in. They carefully placed Bill on a stretcher, his injury clearly taking a toll. The ambulance arrived promptly, and the emergency medical team prepared to transport him to the hospital.

With a final glance back at the scene of chaos, Aury, Luna, and the rest of the group watched as the ambulance pulled away. The night was still filled with flashing lights and the murmur of distant conversations, but the immediate crisis had been averted. As the crowd began to disperse, the sense of relief and the weight of the day's events began to settle in.

# XXXVII
## Chapter 37

**The light on the heart monitor blinked steadily,**
casting a soft glow in the dimly lit hospital room. The steady beep of the machine provided a rhythmic reassurance, a stark contrast to the whirlwind of emotions and events that had unfolded over the past few days.

Bill lay in bed, his chest rising and falling with each labored breath. Aury, ever vigilant, sat beside him, her gaze fixed on his face, her expression a mix of concern and relief. The steady drip of blood from the IV bag into his vein was a reminder of how precarious his condition had been; the doctors had warned that he had lost a significant amount of blood and that the injury was severe, though not life-threatening.

Aury glanced out the window, where the sky was a deep blue, punctuated by the occasional plane carving its path across the sky. A small smile touched her lips as she turned her gaze back to Bill. The sight of him slowly waking brought a fresh wave of hope.

His eyelids fluttered open, and he looked around the room, confusion and recognition battling in his eyes. Aury's heart skipped a beat as she gently placed her hand on his head, her tears glistening as she smiled. "Don't try to get up. You're still weak," she said softly.

Bill's voice was barely above a whisper as he asked, "Where's Luna?"

"She's in the cafeteria with Lara and Amelia. They went to get some ice cream," Aury replied, her voice soothing.

The door creaked open slightly, and a familiar voice floated in from the hallway. "He got a promotion and a month of paid leave," the voice said, followed by a softer, more intimate addition. "But he's also getting a medal from the president in honor." Aury's face lit up with a proud smile, and Bill's cheeks flushed with a mix of embarrassment and happiness.

John peeked through the door, and upon seeing Bill awake, he dashed back into the corridor, probably to rally the others. Moments later, Luna entered the room, her face lighting up with excitement as she carried a large box. John followed, balancing two bottles of champagne, while Lara brought in a bunch of balloons.

Hoffs was right behind, carrying a pack of party poppers. Amelia helped Luna place a cake on the bedside table. The cake, decorated with chocolate icing, read **"For Our SUPER HERO!"** Hud pulled out a lighter and lit the candles, the flames flickering brightly.

The room was soon filled with a cacophony of celebration. Hoffs pulled the string on the party poppers and the room was showered with confetti. The balloons bounced energetically as Hud pinned them to the walls. John poured champagne into plastic glasses, and everyone gathered around Bill, their faces alight with joy and relief.

"To our triumph!" Hoffs declared, raising his glass.

"Cheers!" everyone echoed, their glasses clinking together with a resounding cheer. Bill looked around, his heart swelling with gratitude and love. Hud and Hoffs shared a laugh, while John and Aury playfully fought over the largest piece of cake. Luna, Amelia, and Lara sat together; their camaraderie evident.

Luna noticed Bill's gaze and quickly set her glass aside, her face a mix of shyness and determination. Bill's smile widened as he rolled his eyes playfully. Luna took a deep breath and picked up her glass again, and they shared a tender, silent understanding. Despite the trials and the pain, this was his family—some old, some new, but all vital and supportive.

Aury, seeing the joy in the room, asked gently, "Missing Leo?"

Bill nodded; his smile was bittersweet. His mind drifted back to memories of laughter and camaraderie with Leo, mingled with the heartache of his loss.

The memory of simpler times flashed vividly in Bill's mind. He was back in the old clumsy bar with Leo and Rafi, each of them holding a jug of beer. They laughed uproariously, their camaraderie evident in every hearty laugh and shared joke. But the memory faded, and he found himself back in his small, dimly lit bedroom. The rental house was a far cry from their old, spacious home.

Bill's left hand still ached, a reminder of the pen that had pierced deeply, causing a fracture in his arm. He struggled with his physical limitations but was determined to overcome them. He moved slowly across the cold floor, careful not to disturb Luna, who was sleeping peacefully.

In the study room, Bill sat at the desk cluttered with newspapers and magazines. He flicked on the desk lamp and stared at the computer screen filled with open tabs and images of Leo's village before the attack. "This is how Uncle Leo's village looked before the attack," he explained as Luna, now awake, peered over his shoulder.

"It's so beautiful," Luna marveled at the pictures on the screen.

"Yes, it is," Bill agreed. "And that's why I'm including these pictures in my book. I want people to see what it was like before everything changed."

Luna hesitated for a moment before asking shyly, "Daddy, can we get a puppy again?"

Bill's face lit up with a genuine smile. "Of course we can! I've been thinking about it too."

Luna's eyes sparkled with happiness. "Thank you, Daddy." She hugged him tightly, and Bill's heart swelled with love. In this small, intimate moment, surrounded by the people who mattered most, he found solace and hope for the future.

# THE END

# Acknowledgement

The journey of writing this book has been both challenging and rewarding, and I am fortunate to have had the support of so many wonderful people along the way. This book would not have been possible without your guidance, encouragement, and belief in my vision.

First and foremost, I want to express my deepest gratitude to **Adyant**, whose help was invaluable throughout this entire process. Whether it was brainstorming ideas, offering feedback, or simply being there when I needed advice, your unwavering support made this journey much easier. You have been a constant source of encouragement, and for that, I am deeply thankful.

A special thank you to **Vats Kaushik**, my brilliant editor. Your dedication to refining this manuscript has been nothing short of extraordinary. From the smallest grammatical details to the broader strokes of structure and narrative flow, your insights have elevated this work beyond what I could have achieved on my own. Your patience and thoroughness in editing have made this book stronger, and I'm truly grateful for your expertise.

To **Paulina**, your guidance and wisdom have been invaluable throughout this journey. Your thoughtful advice and your ability to see the bigger picture have helped steer this book in the right direction. You provided clarity when things seemed overwhelming, and your belief in this project was a source of strength.

I am also deeply indebted to my **English teachers**, who have played an integral role in shaping me as a writer. Your passion for language and literature has left an indelible mark on my writing. You taught me to appreciate the power of words and inspired me to pursue storytelling with confidence. I owe much of my love for writing to the lessons I learned in your classrooms.

To **Janvi**, your motivation and positivity have been my driving force. Your belief in my abilities, even when I doubted myself, kept me going. Thank you for always being my first reader and critic.

Your opinions helped me a lot.

I also want to thank all my friends and family for their support, patience, and understanding. You have been my sounding boards, my cheerleaders, and my biggest supporters. Thank you for believing in me and for offering me the space and time I needed to dedicate myself to this work.

Finally, to you, the reader—thank you for choosing to pick up this book. I hope that the stories, ideas, and lessons within these pages resonate with you in some way. Writing is a conversation between the author and the reader, and I hope that this book sparks thoughts, emotions, and perhaps even a new perspective on the topics it explores.

With immense gratitude,
Davit Shyam

# ACKNOWLEDGEMENT

# About The Author

**Davit Shyam** is a young and enthusiastic writer whose passion for storytelling has been a constant companion throughout his life. Currently a high school student, Davit has always been drawn to the power of words, starting his journey by writing poetry and short stories for school magazines. What began as a creative outlet during school assignments soon transformed into a deeper love for literature and storytelling, sparking his ambition to write more extensive works.

Like many his age, Davit enjoys reading books and playing games, but writing holds a special place in his heart. For him, the process of crafting stories is not only a source of joy but also a form of relaxation, providing an escape from the stresses of daily life. Despite the challenges of balancing schoolwork, extracurricular activities, and personal life, Davit is committed to nurturing his craft. Each day, no matter how busy, he makes it a point to carve out time for writing, finding inspiration in everything from his everyday experiences to the books he reads and the games he plays.

Writing, for Davit, is not just about putting words on paper; it's about exploring ideas, emotions, and the world around him. His storytelling reflects his unique perspective as a young writer, capturing both the simplicity and complexity of life through his youthful lens. This book, his first, is a culmination of his early years of learning, growth, and exploration as a writer.

With this debut, Davit hopes to connect with readers on a deeper level and inspire them with his stories, just as many authors have inspired him. He views this book not only as a milestone in his writing journey but also as the beginning of what he hopes will be a long and fulfilling career as an author.